THE URBANA FREE LIBRARY

W9-BDV-511

The Urbana Free Library

To renew materials call
217-367-4057

DISCARDED BY THE
URBANA FREE LIBRARY

DATE DUE		
APR 2 8 2010		
JAN 2 8 2011		

cuRes *for* heArtbreAk

URBANA FREE LIBRARY

cuRes
for
heartbreAk

MARGO RABB

URBANA FREE LIBRARY

DELACORTE PRESS

Published by Delacorte Press
an imprint of Random House Children's Books
a division of Random House, Inc.
New York

This is a work of fiction. Names, characters, places, and incidents either
are the product of the author's imagination or are used fictitiously. Any
resemblance to actual persons, living or dead, events, or locales is
entirely coincidental.

Copyright © 2007 by Margo Rabb

"How to Survive a Funeral" was published in significantly different form under the title "Black
Humor" in *Seventeen,* August 2000; a revised section of the story also appeared under the title
"Ghost Story" in *One Story,* Issue 24, 2003.

"World History" was published in different form in the anthology *American Fiction: The Best
Unpublished Stories by Emerging Writers,* 9th Edition, Minneapolis:
New Rivers Press, 1997.

"Hospital Food" appeared in significantly different form under the title "Rearranging My
Heart" in *Seventeen,* May 1997.

"My Mother's First Love" was published in different form under the title
"My Mother's First Lover" in *The Atlantic Monthly,* November 1998, and reprinted in *Best New
American Voices,* 2000.

"How to Find Love" was published in different form in *Glimmer Train Stories,* Winter 2000, and
reprinted in *Mother Knows: 24 Tales of Motherhood,*
New York: Simon & Schuster, 2004.

Brief excerpt from "How to Find Love" segment adapted from *Having It All,* published by
Simon & Schuster, copyright © 1982 by Helen Gurley Brown.

"Seduce Me" was published in different form under the title "Fortune" in *Shenandoah,* Summer
2002, and published in significantly different form in *Seventeen,* December 2001.

All rights reserved.

Delacorte Press and colophon are registered trademarks of
Random House, Inc.

www.randomhouse.com/teens

Educators and librarians, for a variety of teaching tools, visit us at
www.randomhouse.com/teachers

Library of Congress Cataloging-in-Publication Data
Rabb, M. E.
Cures for heartbreak / Margo Rabb. – 1st ed.
p. cm.
Summary: As she navigates adolescence, ninth-grader Mia must deal with her
mother's recent death and her father's illness while she searches for friendship
and love in the world around her.
ISBN 978-0-385-73402-8 (hc) – ISBN 978-0-385-90414-8 (glb)
[1. Parent and child–Fiction. 2. Death–Fiction. 3. Interpersonal relations–Fiction.
4. New York (N.Y.)–Fiction.] I. Title.
PZ7.R1032Cu 2007
[Fic]–dc22
2006007333

Printed in the United States of America

10 9 8 7 6 5 4 3 2 1

First Edition

To the memory of my parents,
Renée and Steve Rabb

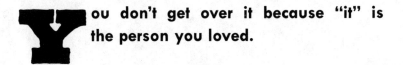**Y**ou don't get over it because "it" is the person you loved.

—Jeanette Winterson
Written on the Body

contents

Contents

How to Survive a Funeral

disbelieving, we endured the wreath on the door, and the undertaker coming and going, the influx of food, the overpowering odor of white flowers, and all the rest of it . . . my father was all but undone by my mother's death. . . . I overheard one family friend after another assuring him that there was no cure but time, and though he said, "Yes, I know," I could tell he didn't believe them . . . what the family friends said is true. For some people. For others the hands of the clock can go round till kingdom come and not cure anything.

—William Maxwell
So Long, See You Tomorrow

The Host

THE FUNERAL DIRECTOR'S name was Manny Musico.

"Is that like a stage name?" my sister, Alex, asked.

"No," he said proudly. "It's real." The gel in his black curls glistened; his teeth sparkled in the artificial light. He was good-looking in a soap opera way and seemed young for his profession.

I leaned over to my sister and whispered, "What a morbid job."

Manny also had supersonic hearing. "A lot of people think so, but it's not morbid at all!" His voice boomed like a Broadway star's; he adjusted his lapels and beamed. I wouldn't have been entirely shocked if spotlights had flicked on, coffins opened up, dancing corpses emerged, and Manny led us all in the opening number of *Funeral!*, the musical.

"Getting down to business," Manny said, "can I please have the death certificate?"

My father handed it to him and recounted the details about our mother—a sudden death, twelve days after the diagnosis; no, no one expected it; he was sorry too. Forms were filled out. Then Manny invited us to view the coffins.

"She went into the hospital with a stomachache," my dad continued as Manny led us downstairs and along a wood-paneled corridor to the coffin vault.

Manny said, "We've gotten some new models in."

The coffins: luxury models lined with silk, the plain pine box preferred by the Orthodox. My eyes bulged at the prices. A thousand dollars. Two thousand. Four thousand. The caskets had names–Abraham, Eleazar, Moses, Shalom.

"How about the Eleazar?" my father asked. The Eleazar cost $1,699.

"It looks okay," I said. This could not be happening. Oak finish. Satin-lined. "Are we going to get the Star of David on top?"

"I think it costs extra. But what the hell. I think Omi and Opa would want it." Omi and Opa were my mother's parents.

"We don't need the fucking star," my sister growled.

Manny decided to leave us alone with the coffins. "I'll give you some time to decide."

My father examined the finish of the Abraham and said for the fifth time in two days, "We're in a play in which the funeral is the last act," in his usual deadpan tone.

"That's new," Alex snapped. "Did you get that out of a book or something?"

"He can repeat it if he wants to," I said.

She glared at me. "Mia thinks we are in a play–rated triple X. Did you see her this morning?" she asked our father. "She was trying on a slutty dress to wear to the funeral."

"It wasn't a slutty dress." It was a velvet halter dress I'd recently worn to a sweet sixteen. I touched the shiny handle of

6

the $4,000 mahogany Shalom. "It's my only black dress. It's not like I wanted to wear pasties and a G-string."

"I wouldn't be surprised if you did."

"Shut up."

"You shut up."

"*You* shut up."

"*Girls,*" our father said. "Please. Girls. After this, we'll go shopping."

This was a shock, since he found shopping as enjoyable as setting himself on fire.

Manny poked his head in. "Everything okay?"

"Fine," my father said. "We'll take the Eleazar, with the Star of David." He answered more questions, signed some paperwork, and as we got ready to leave, he told Manny we were off to Bloomingdale's.

"Have fun," Manny called after us.

The Shopping Trip

My father pulled up to a hydrant a block from Bloomingdale's. "I'll wait here, save on parking," he said, and unfurled his beloved *New York Times*. He handed my sister his credit card like it was a rare gem.

To my mother and me, Bloomingdale's was a spiritual

homeland. I worshipped those dresses on the mannequins in the windows, the bright pocketbooks swinging on silver racks, and the gleaming sky-high stilettos. Every time we shopped there, I'd inhale the heady perfumes and sweet chemical scent of brand-new clothes as my mother and I scanned the store for deities (she'd once sighted Marilyn Monroe at the Chanel counter, and I'd seen Molly Ringwald in Shoes on 2.) Then we'd ogle the merchandise.

We'd try not to buy too much (so my father wouldn't kill us), but we'd soon find ourselves happily cascading up the escalator with a big brown bag of on-sale skirts, barrettes, panty hose, underwear, and of course Estée Lauder products that were accompanied by free gifts. My mother hoarded these free bonuses–lacquered boxes, makeup kits, tote bags, pocket mirrors.

My sister had never been part of our shopping trips. Now I watched her galumph down the aisles in her hiking boots, jeans, and Mets jersey, digging through the racks and making faces at the clothes. Her hair frizzed around her head like a dandelion.

"I'll be in Dresses," I said. I walked over to that section and there I saw it on the sale rack. Cap-sleeved chiffon with an embroidered overlay; I'd tried on this dress two months before with my mother. We hadn't bought it–it was $149–but I'd fallen for this dress. We'd oohed and aahed. We'd held our breath, fingering the embroidery.

I stared at the price tag: $119 on sale. Not much of an improvement.

I eyed the skinny girls with pink backpacks browsing the racks and thought, *My mother would want me to have this dress.* Maybe she'd left the dress here, in fact, for me to wear. Maybe it was a sign.

I walked over to my sister, who was holding black pants and a matching shirt. "Guess I'll get this," she sighed, as if buying them would cause her physical pain. She stared at the dress draped over my arm. "Is that a scarf?"

"It's a dress."

"It's see-through."

"It's not."

"It's snot?"

I rolled my eyes.

"How much?" she asked.

I shrugged. "Not much."

She lifted the price tag. "*One hundred and nineteen?* What is that, drachmas? Shekels?"

"I'm getting it," I said.

Her voice rose. "You're not paying a hundred and nineteen dollars for a scarf!"

The customers on line gaped at us. "It's for Mommy's *funeral,*" I said. "I think a nice dress is worth it for Mommy's *funeral.*" As soon as the words were out I wished I hadn't said them. My entire life had become a CBS Sunday Night Movie, and it was only getting worse.

Her eyes flashed. "There's no way we're buying that dress!"

I threw it on the counter. "Fine. Forget it." My throat dried up. I marched off to the escalator.

I rode it down to Hosiery and wandered around the panty hose. I could run away. Where would I go? Upstate? The wilderness? I imagined riding Metro-North and getting off at the last stop, wherever that was, and starting a new life. Ten minutes later I headed out the main door in the vague direction of Grand Central Station.

Alex was waiting on the sidewalk. I ignored her and hurried up the street.

"Here's your stupid dress," she said from behind me, waving the shopping bag at me. I walked away from her; she caught up. I walked faster; she did too. I started running, and she chased after me; I arrived at the car out of breath, ahead of her.

"I got here first," I said inanely, as if I needed to prove I'd won the pre-funeral foot race, an ancient ceremonial Jewish tradition.

Is God a Comedian from the Borscht Belt?

My mother had told us the diagnosis herself, the first night she was in the hospital. We were all there, my father, Alex, and me, at the foot of my mother's bed, sitting there awkwardly, trying to pretend this was a natural, normal family situation, the three of us hanging around her hospital bed.

"Well." She smiled. "Melanoma."

She shrugged. And smiled again, as if it was amusing, as if

she really wanted to say, *Ha! Isn't this funny? Cancer. I thought I had a stomachache.*

We all sort of smiled then, the four of us with these sick, manic, dumb, painfully goofy smiles, because we didn't know what else to do. It was like a Norman Rockwell painting gone awry–*Gee, Mom's got Cancer!*–and our frozen, psychotic grins.

Then the four of us went to the solarium, and Alex and I talked about school, grades, Alex's senior-year research paper on isotopes, my new nail polish. A normal conversation, things would be normal. The cancer had metastasized to my mother's liver. "You never know what can happen," a nurse told us later. "Remain hopeful."

I didn't know it that night, but that was the last normal conversation I'd have with my mother. Perhaps this was why I replayed the diagnosis scene so often in my head in the days leading up to the funeral, trying to understand it, to revise it, to make myself say something important, *anything*.

I'd waited to cry until I'd gotten in bed that night. I cried till I ran out of tears, and then I lay there and could feel my insides churning. I hadn't known that it would be such a tangible, physical pain, yet so much worse than anything that was only physical. My insides churned and churned as if machines were methodically grinding my inner organs to a pulp. I used to think the worst pain I'd ever felt was one summer when I'd slipped on wet leaves in the alley behind our house and broke my arm. Now I wanted to laugh at my own stupidity. I'd thought *that* had hurt?

The day before my mother died they moved her into a room with another woman who was dying. Mrs. Flemsky was much older; her husband stood vigil by her bed and her children came to visit, but they were decades older than Alex and me, married and with a heap of their own children. When no one was around, Mrs. Flemsky liked to chant Yiddish in a vaguely musical tone. "Oy gevalt oy gevalt oygevaltoygevalt. Oy oy oy oyoyoyoyoyoyoy" in a constant refrain. Alex had pinched me in the side and led me to the solarium.

"I had to get out of there," she said. "It's like Intro to Yiddish. Yiddish 101."

"Like a cappella klezmer music," I said.

"Oyoyoy," my sister sang.

We laughed, but it wasn't a regular kind of laugh; it almost felt like throwing up. We'd been laughing like this frequently in the hospital. We'd laughed when the old woman who shared our mother's room in the ICU a week ago moaned, "Who took my bladder? Where did my bladder go?" and at the smiling, toothless man who paraded down the hall with his gown half open and his butt hanging out. Then there was the nearly blind lady who roamed the solarium, trailing her IV behind her like a pet on a leash. "Hymie? Hymie, is that you?" she once asked me.

We'd even laughed after we overheard our father's cardiologist telling one of our father's friends that because of his heart disease, he had a 50 percent chance of dying within the next year, from the stress of losing a spouse. "We better sign up at the orphanage now, ha ha ha!" Alex had said.

The Rabbi

When the rabbi arrived we realized God was definitely a comedian from the Borscht Belt.

Since we weren't religious we didn't have our own rabbi; Manny ordered one for us. The day of the funeral, Rabbi Rosenbaum arrived wearing gold rings and Ray-Bans, his shirt unbuttoned a third of the way down to reveal a hairy triangle of rabbinical chest.

"Figures," Alex whispered. "We got Rabbi Elvis."

He looked through the forms on his desk. "Okay. Okay. Whatta we got here." He squinted at the paper. "Greta. Greta Rivkah Pearlman. Date of death January seventeenth, 1991. Am I saying her name correctly? No uncommon pronunciations?"

We shook our heads.

He reviewed all our names and our mother's history, date of birth, et cetera, and entered them on his prepared form. "Adjective?" I expected him to ask next, as if he was filling out a Mad Lib.

Before the funeral began, Manny said, "You can take a few moments alone with her if you like." None of us wanted to look at the casket. Finally, my father said he'd do it while my sister and I waited in the hall.

"She looks okay," my father said. "It looks like her. They did a nice job."

This could not be happening.

So many people arrived that we had to switch chapels to a larger one—there was my mother's whole department from work; Fanny Gluckman, my mother's best friend, who'd moved away four years ago; Mrs. Kopecki, the Lillys and Lombardis, and other neighbors from our block. Rabbi Rosenbaum seemed pleased that he'd have a larger audience. After everyone was seated he ushered us down the aisle and to the front pew.

The service itself passed quickly, the Hebrew prayers I didn't understand, the standing up, the sitting down; I wasn't sure what it had to do with my mother. My father, sister, and I were all too stunned to give speeches, but Opa, my German grandfather, who ordinarily barely said a word, uttered a few sentences in Hebrew, which hardly anybody understood.

"Yitgadal v'yitkadash," the rabbi chanted. I wanted to join in the mourner's prayer, but I didn't know it. For almost two weeks now I'd recorded everything that happened in the pink journal my mom had given me for my fifteenth birthday, as if writing it down was the only way to make it real, to figure out how I felt and what to do. The night of the diagnosis, I'd scribbled: *If she dies, I'll die.*

I stared at the hem of my $119 dress and thought about the one night I'd left the hospital to go home and instead of getting on the 4 train at 33rd Street, I walked all the way to the Barnes & Noble on 54th. I kept walking and when I got there I scanned the shelves of the grief section, the Death & Dying shelves, for a book that would comfort me, that would say exactly the right thing. I'm not sure what I'd been looking for, exactly. Maybe something like *What to Do When Your Mother Dies from Melanoma, Which They Thought Was a*

Stomachache at First. How to Cope When You're Left Alone
with Your Father and Sister, Who Drive You Nuts. How to
Survive a Funeral, Especially One Hosted by a Disconcertingly
Happy Funeral Director and an Upwardly Mobile Rabbi Who
Drives a BMW. I didn't find a book I wanted to buy. All that
had made me feel better was the walk.

The Boy

After the service, we were ushered out to the limousine
briskly and on to the cemetery, and before I knew it we were
home.

For hours we sat like mannequins, greeting the parade of
sympathizers. There were people I hadn't seen in years, people
I'd forgotten existed: Mrs. Lowery, my kindergarten teacher;
Dr. Book, our orthodontist; Lottie Silverberg, my babysitter
when I was six. I'd almost stopped being surprised at who
appeared when Jay Kasper, a senior at our school, strode
through the door.

My stomach jumped: he was the demigod of the Bronx
High School of Science. He was Alex's year but she didn't know
him, and she thought it was ridiculous that my freshman
friends and I often trekked to Central Park to swoon and fanta-
size while he played ultimate Frisbee. His father was a partner
at the law firm where my mother was a paralegal, but we'd

never spoken, except for one brief exchange on the subway: "You got gum?" he'd asked me and my friends. Ten packets of Wrigley's had been proffered instantaneously.

Mr. Kasper gave us his condolences; Mrs. Kasper clasped my hands and stared at me as if I was an abandoned kitten she wanted to stuff into her pocketbook.

Then came Jay. He stood before me, clutching a silver baking pan. Our eyes locked. "I brought you this," he said. The pan was filled with melted brown crayons.

"Wow, thanks."

"They're Rice Krispies treats. Made with Cocoa Krispies, that is."

I set the pan down beside the coffee urns, and Jay handed me a treat. I crunched into it. It stuck to my teeth. We stood there, chewing.

"This is good," I said.

"Yeah." He inspected a Cocoa Krispies treat thoughtfully, then looked at me. "You know I spent last summer in Kenya? Studying wildlife and stuff? They have parties there when someone dies. To celebrate that they're in a better place."

"Really? Huh. I didn't know." We were silent for several minutes; I wasn't sure what to say. All I could think was, *Jay Kasper is standing beside me. Jay Kasper is in my house.* With him next to me, his voice so close to my face, the brick lodged in my chest loosened a little; for a moment I forgot it existed. In its place was this other person, and I wondered at how life did that, how in its bleakest moments the world coughed up somebody new.

"Hey—I like your dress," he said. "I mean—it looks good. Nice. Black."

Alex rushed over from the tray of cold cuts.

"*Mia.* We *need* you. In the *kitchen.*" She whisked me into our tiny kitchen, nearly pinning me to the refrigerator.

"What?"

"You know, you're really *sick.*"

"What am I doing?"

"You're flirting with this guy minutes after Mommy's funeral." She shook her head, exasperated. I closed my eyes and envisioned the sister I often dreamed of–tall and blond and 34C, wise to the secrets of eye shadow application, French kissing, hair removal. But when I opened my eyes it was still Alex, saying, "Why don't you skip the pretenses and just take him to bed?"

"Why don't you shut the fuck up?"

Several heads peeked down the hall; the voices in the living room froze. My father, still clumsy in his new single-parenting role, trudged awkwardly into the kitchen to ordain peace.

"Girls. What's the matter?"

"Mia is a *bitch* is what's the matter."

Fanny Gluckman padded in. Her daughter Lucy had been my best friend before they moved away, but we hadn't been in touch lately; Lucy had left a message on our answering machine three days ago saying she was sorry, but she couldn't make it to the funeral. A part of me hadn't wanted anyone to come to the funeral, to witness the horror that had formerly been our normal lives–and another part wanted everybody I'd ever met to be there, because the more people who came, and the longer they stayed, the less real it all seemed.

Fanny carried a Barnes & Noble tote bag, which she never put down. A tarnished Star of David hung from her throat.

"Girls, let's think of your mother right now. Greta wouldn't want you to be fighting. It's important that we keep thinking of what your mother would want. When a family sits shiva—not that you're doing that, exactly—but the point behind the traditions, of covering the mirrors, not wearing any makeup, not fighting with each other, is to think of the person who died. Not of yourselves."

Alex and I avoided each other's gaze and returned to the living room; things seemed pacified until Jay came up to me to say good-bye.

"Hey? Hey. You know, the Hellmonkeys are playing at CB's Friday. I mean—I bet you wouldn't want to see them with me."

"Friday?"

"I mean, I'm sure with everything you wouldn't want to. It wouldn't be right. Forget—"

"No—I would. I love the Hellmonkeys. I'd love to go."

"She's *disgusting*," Alex said to our father when the only visitors left were my mother's silent, dazed parents, staring blankly at their stained and empty coffee cups, and Fanny, wrapping up the casseroles.

"It's not disgusting," my father said diplomatically. "It'll be good for your sister to see a performance that she likes. If she wants to get out of the house, she can go."

Alex glared at me as we cleared the tables.

"You know, in Kenya they have huge parties after someone dies," I said. "One big fucking party."

She banged the dishes into the sink. "This isn't Kenya, Mia, this is Queens. Stop saying *fuck*."

"You say it."

"That's different. I'm older."

"Enough," Fanny shouted, her mouth full of fruitcake. "Let's put a stop to this now. Alex, Mia, come here." She took each of our hands. "Tell each other 'I love you.' "

"I love you," Alex whispered with remarkable hostility.

"I love *you*," I snapped.

"That's a start," Fanny said.

The Musical Show

Jay Kasper picked me up in his parents' Astro van. I wore my velvet halter dress; my sister's gaze drilled into my bare shoulders. She and my father said good-bye to us from the couch, where they'd settled in for a thrilling evening of *This Old House* repeats.

On the drive over the 59th Street Bridge I kept thinking that Jay had been sent to me for a reason. "There's a reason for everything," Fanny had told me on the phone while my mom was in the hospital. *What reason?* I'd wanted to ask. *What? What could the reason possibly be?*

Now I thought: *If God was a comedian from the Borscht Belt, He would want me to go on a date to a club shortly after my mom's funeral. In fact, He probably planned it this way.* Like the dress, Jay Kasper had been sent to me. For a reason.

We parked on 7th Street and walked past the night crowds

and litter and homeless people leaning on parking meters, over to the Bowery.

We saw other people from school at the club—Mallory Diaz, Maria Heller, Gloria Morales—the senior girls my friends and I always admired from afar, with their silky dark hair, black tights, and the matching high-heeled black boots I coveted. Where they bought those boots I didn't know, though I'd searched for them in Bloomingdale's and nearly every store on 8th Street. Those girls' outfits always seemed put together with a perfection I never could master—even when I wore what I thought was the perfect dress, my tights always seemed to bag at the ankles, my shoes got scuffed, my hair blew into creative sculptures.

The girls eyed me up and down as Jay led me through the crowd. The music pounded. "It's a really good band," he said. The song was called "Morning Breath" and, Jay explained, was about the lead singer's ex-girlfriend.

"Morning breath!" the lead Hellmonkey screamed. "She's got morning-morning-morning breath!"

The crowd chanted. Boys dove off the stage. "Hey—you having fun?" Jay shouted.

"Yeah! Lots." I wasn't really having fun; it was something else entirely, something not quite fun but not exactly misery either. His arm brushed mine; he turned to me every few seconds and grinned. I tried to look confident and assured, as if the two of us here together was a perfectly natural thing. I worried that my mother's death showed all over my body, visible in my hair and on my forehead, seeping out of my velvet dress, the same dress I'd worn when I'd come home late two months ago from my neighbor Rita Kircher's sweet sixteen. My mom had waited up, and we'd sat at the kitchen table eating Entenmann's pound cake as I told her about the party.

Midway through the show, Mallory and Gloria came over to us. "You know Mia?" Jay asked them.

They smiled politely at me, as if I was his grandmother, and pulled him aside. I couldn't hear what they said; they excused themselves and took Jay with them, to talk to somebody else. I stood there alone, jostled between six-foot-tall boys with blue hair and girls with spiked belts, stuck in a forest of sweaty skinny metal-studded humans. I pretended to enjoy myself. I was about to escape to the bathroom when an overgrown limb knocked into me, spilling an entire beer down my dress.

"Oops," a guy in a Megadeath T-shirt said. He smirked.

I stared down at my dress, at the crushed and dripping velvet. Sometimes my mother used to tell me—when I came home from school with a ketchup stain on a white shirt, or when she glanced into my room and saw herds of sweaters amassing on the floor—that I should take better care of my clothes. I'd never really cared that much, as clothes had always seemed replaceable. Now every grocery list and doodle on a Post-it and frozen pound cake and dress that my mother had touched had a spell cast on it. She'd hugged me in this dress.

I burrowed my way through the crowd to the bathroom and stood by the sink rubbing the dress, *dry clean only* running through my head. Alex had mumbled to me earlier that night: "That's really nice that you're going out partying right after Mommy died." I'd told her to go to hell, but a part of me had known that she was right. I'd justified it by thinking that I was only trying to make myself feel better.

After all, wasn't that what this was all about? The funeral, Manny Musico, the rabbi, the visitors and flowers and cards– wasn't everyone just trying to make us feel better? Of course, death was probably the only thing in the world that couldn't be made better. Obviously, she wasn't coming back.

I made my way through the crowd to Jay, who stood by the side of the stage, and told him I wanted to go.

"What happened? What's wrong?"

"Nothing. I'm just tired; I just want to go home." I didn't really want to go home; I just couldn't think of anywhere else to go.

He drove me home. We barely spoke the whole way. I watched the sparse midnight traffic, listened to the groans of the subway overhead. On my stoop he leaned against the railing. "Hey–I hoped this would cheer you up. My mom thought it would be a good thing. I mean–you had fun, right?"

I nodded. I smelled like a keg. I didn't know going out had been his mother's idea.

When I used to watch after-school specials I'd wanted to be that girl–the one the special was about, the girl with some terrible disease or the sufferer of some noble catastrophe. Pitied and loved. Of course in real life the pity, or whatever it was, was nothing like the way it seemed on the show; it resulted not in reverence but in something more like humiliation. I was ashamed of my family for having such bad luck. Who dies in twelve days?

He smiled and turned to go, then stopped. "Hey. I wanted to tell you. I'm real sorry you're so sad."

"Oh. Thanks." Sad? I wanted to tear my skin off or run screaming down the street.

"I wish I could help," he said.

I stared at the red concrete of our stoop. "I just want someone to tell me what to do."

"What?" he asked.

I meant that I wanted to know how you dealt with this, with the worst thing. "I mean . . . Forget it. See you in school," I said.

"Okay. See you in school."

I shut the door and walked into the silent emptiness of our house. It felt like a different house. There was nobody waiting up. The furniture looked old and worn, the floors dirty, the kitchen table barely visible beneath the pile of cards that needed to be answered. The flowers and flowers and flowers.

I went upstairs to my room. I didn't undress. I collapsed on my bed and listened to the cars whirring down our street, a fire engine squealing in the distance. I stayed awake for a long time, counting the spots on the ceiling where the paint had peeled off. After a while I got up and went into my parents' room.

My sister was already there. My father snored on my mother's old side of the bed; my sister slept in my father's spot.

I poked her. "Move over." She grumbled unintelligibly and moved over an inch. I poked her again. She groaned and moved further. I squeezed into the little slice of mattress, nudging her over, pulling the old flowered comforter up beneath my chin. I stared at the shadows on the ceiling that I'd stared at my whole life.

If she dies, I'll die. But here we were.

World History

istory . . . isn't simply what has happened. It's a judgment on what has happened.

—Cynthia Ozick
Trust

FOUR DAYS AFTER the funeral, my father decided that Alex and I should go back to school. I was reading in bed when he knocked on my door, peered into my room, and repeated, as he'd been doing at regular intervals, like a public service announcement, that we needed to go back to the way things were before. On Monday he'd reopen his shoe repair shop, I'd return to the ninth grade, and Alex to the twelfth. Things had to go back to normal.

I stared up at him from my *Anne of Green Gables*. I was entranced by every orphan book I could find–*Heidi, Oliver Twist, The Secret Garden*–like they were company. The stream of visitors had petered out to just a few neighbors and the occasional oddity, such as Melody Bly, a religious girl in my class who had come in bearing a card signed by our homeroom and history teacher, Mr. Flag, and thirty-one classmates. The card had a huge gold cross on the front; at first glance I thought it was a plus sign. I'd barely ever spoken to Melody; she gave me a book called *The Five Stages of Grief,* filled with hazy photographs of silhouettes gazing out windows. I'd stuck it on the kitchen table on top of all the other cards we'd received, with their wispy watercolor flowers, sunrises, beach scenes, and vague quotes in curlicue scripts.

Though a tree may lose its limb, new boughs will grow and shade the empty space.

Grieve but a day—spend your lifetime celebrating the love you shared.

Love . . . bright as sunshine.
Loss . . . large as the ocean deep.
Time . . . will heal your heartbreak.
Memories . . . will bring you peace.

"I got peanut butter," my father said. He hovered in the doorway and gazed at me in my twin bed. "I'll make your lunch for tomorrow." He never made my lunch; I made it myself. And he rarely came into my room. Though I'd hardly changed anything since I was ten, he looked around it now like he was seeing it for the first time: the mobile of satiny stars above my door; my shelf of Barbies, scantily clad in bikinis made from old tights; a poster of Rob Lowe with lipstick marks on his bare chest; the menagerie of stuffed animals I'd loved all my life, their fur matted, faces flat as pancakes from years of being slept on. In a sudden wash of maturity two years ago I'd put them all in the closet, but in the last couple of weeks I'd taken them out and stationed them around my bed, like a plush army.

My father's eyes focused on a shelf by the window. A yahrzeit candle stood beside the Barbies. When Manny Musico had offered the candle to us my father had refused it, but as we were leaving I'd asked if I could have it. I hadn't known what a yahrzeit candle was, but I'd wanted it. I'd taken everything Manny offered us—the Schwartz Memorial Chapel stationery, the gold-embossed guestbook, the Hebrew prayer cards—all of it tucked into the Schwartz Memorial Chapel bag, like party favors.

The candle was still burning. The instruction booklet it came with said not to blow it out, that it would last for seven days to represent the formal mourning period. I'd been blowing it out at night anyway because I was afraid of burning down the house. And secretly I wanted it to last longer.

My father kept staring at the candle. He'd never been exactly euphoric over the idea of religion. He'd repeat "Religion Is the Cause of All the World's Ills" as often as "Don't Throw Out the Milk Without Letting Your Father Sniff It First." His idea of marking Yom Kippur was to eat smoked kippers. My mother wasn't too fond of religion either—she and her best friend, Fanny, used to tell the story of how a Catholic friend in elementary school once suggested: "Let's go to your church and then to mine!" The Catholic church had been filled with flowers, singing, smiling . . . and then they went on to my mother and Fanny's Orthodox synagogue, crowded with all the other German Jewish refugee families in Washington Heights who'd narrowly escaped the Holocaust. My mother had been a baby when she and her parents fled Berlin in 1939, on one of the last boats America let in; Fanny's family had come from Amsterdam. That day in the synagogue, the girls had to sit upstairs in the cold darkness, enduring the musty smell, listening to the solemn Hebrew words–they giggled until they got asked to leave.

Because of my parents' profound distaste for going to synagogue, and rarely taking me to one, my notion of the Jewish religion mainly revolved around food. Rosh Hashanah: apples and honey cake, for a sweet New Year. Yom Kippur: instead of the customary fasting to atone for your sins, we atoned with smoked fish in all its glorious variations, from the aforementioned kippers to sable to lox to whitefish to herring. Chanukah, the festival of lights and fried foods: latkes glistening with oil, applesauce and sour cream on the side. Passover: matzo sandwiches, matzo brei, and matzo ball soup to commemorate our ancestors' quick exodus from Egypt (no time for the bread to rise). According to Alex, our culinary version of Judaism meant we weren't Jewish at all. I maintained we were, though I wondered privately if she was right.

My father adjusted his glasses and leaned against the door. "You'll enjoy being back at school."

I pictured my teachers, lined up like the cast of *The Addams Family,* their ghoulish faces cackling–Mrs. Petrosky, the sadistic Russian physicist; Mr. O'Grady, who sipped from a flask between classes and had a penchant for Korean girls; Mr. Tortolano, my English teacher, who, rumor had it, was an upstanding member of the North American Man-Boy Love Association; and Mr. Flag. Oh, Mr. Flag. Joe Randazzo, who sat next to me in history, circulated a drawing of Mr. Flag, appropriately named, his stiff facial expressions explained by a large flagpole up his rear end.

I couldn't imagine myself back in the classroom beside

Melody and Joe and Petrosky and Flag. I hadn't exactly found my crowd at the Bronx High School of Science yet. Just girls like Eva Friedman and Lana Hernandez, who I hung out with at lunch and rode the train home with. I was waiting for a real best friend, someone who'd come into my life and share all my secrets, someone I could tell everything to, the way I used to with Lucy Gluckman. After the funeral, Eva's and Lana's eyes had searched me with a horrified fascination, as if my mother's death might show physically, like a huge wart or missing limb. "Uh, sorry," Eva had said. Not that I knew what to say either. What could I say? *New boughs are growing. Memories are bringing me peace.*

"You'll feel better once things are normal again," my father said in the doorway.

He stared at the puffy stars dangling above his head and pinched one, as if testing whether it was real. His glasses were as thick as storm windows, his face expressionless. "Stoneface," my mother used to call him, in a not-so-joking tone. "Talk back! Speak to me!" she'd scream at him, and he'd slump on the couch and not respond. No matter what my parents talked about–the telephone bill, cleaning the gerbil cage, who'd bought the scratchy brand of toilet paper–they'd fight. They'd even fought in the hospital: my father wanted to bring my mother's parents to see her, and she refused. She'd never gotten along with her parents, and she didn't want to see them now. One afternoon my father had pulled my sister and me into the hospital corridor and said, "I'm bringing Omi and Opa."

"Why?" I'd asked. My mother had seemed miserable enough already.

"Mommy doesn't understand Omi and Opa. That's the problem. She's never accepted all they've been through." *All they've been through* hung in the air above us heavily, unexplained, like everything from my mother's life: her swastika-stamped birth certificate shoved in her dresser drawer; the space on the family tree my sister once drew for class, with question marks where our mother's aunts, uncles, and cousins should be. After several phone calls to my grandparents, Alex had found out a few facts to add–the places of death for our great-grandparents and two cousins. Bergen-Belsen, Theresienstadt. My grandparents didn't know the dates. Alex penciled the concentration camp names in on her strange and stunted drawing, a sickly tree with empty limbs.

Omi and Opa still lived in Washington Heights, but they didn't get a chance to see my mother before she died. It had happened so surprisingly quickly–my father hadn't arranged their visit in time. At the funeral I'd stared at Omi beside me on the pew in her heaping wig, and Opa steadying himself with his cane; I'd wanted to extract my mother from them, whatever part of her that they held. They spoke little except for a few exchanges in German to each other.

My father called them nightly now. His own Polish-born parents were long dead, his aunts and uncles relocated to Yonkers; only my sister, father, and I remained in Queens, half a block down from where my father had grown up.

"I'll wake you up at six-fifteen," he said, and shut the door. I groaned. I'd been sleeping until noon every day, waking in a coma-like state. I dreaded getting up when it was still dark, to wait on the icy 7 train platform for the hour-and-fifteen-minute subway ride to school. I hated being smushed in the train car with dozens of commuters sweating in their winter coats, grumbling in ten different languages, reaching desperately for the silver poles as the train squealed and tilted like it was about to topple off the tracks.

"I'm glad I'm going back," Alex said during our nightly attack of the post-funeral food supply. She dug into a half-destroyed strudel; I ate the frosting off a cupcake. "It's better than moping here."

"I like moping." I didn't want to face the level buzz of the lunchroom and the day packaged neatly into its eight periods, and I shuddered at the thought of seeing Jay Kasper; I hoped he hadn't told people about our pity date. But I wrapped up a cupcake and a piece of strudel to take to lunch the next day. My father made us peanut butter and jelly sandwiches.

That night I dreamed I was back at school, telling everyone that my mom had died. In the dream they all said, "So what?"

The Bronx High School of Science is a sprawling 1950s architectural monstrosity of glass and red brick, several long, cold blocks from the Bedford Park Boulevard stop on the D train. It was early February; the wind whipped down the wide, deserted streets. I walked past the railway yard and Harris Field, which looked less like a field and more like an abandoned lot.

My first-period class was history. I settled into my assigned seat between Nagma Pawa and Joe Randazzo. We sat in welded-down rows, beside the barred windows. (Were

35

they afraid we'd steal the desks, or jump out?) No one paid attention to me being back after the long absence. No one mentioned my mother. I felt partly relieved but partly disappointed. I didn't know what I'd expected, but I had expected something. Alex would probably say, *Did you think you deserved a parade?*

"Pearlman. Long time no see," Joe said.

"Yeah," I said.

Melody clicked over in her patent leather Mary Janes. She wore tiny silver cross earrings and a corduroy jumper. Her fashion taste lingered in the era of OshKosh and Underoos. "How are *you?*" she asked, gazing at me like she wanted to shrink-wrap me and take me home as her own grief specimen.

"Fine." I took out my notebook, turned away from her, and started to doodle.

Mr. Flag took attendance. He looked like a businessman who'd wandered into the classroom on his way to the office. He wore suits with creased pants, pristine white shirts, and tasteful ties, unlike our other teachers. Their shirts seemed permanently untucked, the soles were peeling off their ratty sneakers, and their ties, on the rare occasions they wore them, featured smiling squirrels or dancing pencils. Mr. Flag revered the meticulous Delaney attendance-taking system—little pink and white cards, which he marked up with the four-colored pen he kept clipped to his inside pocket. I could see my card on his desk, scarred in red.

Mr. Flag was additionally unique in that he swore by the Study Skills Acquisition Program, color-coded packets that corresponded to our textbook, which required writing long, dull answers to longer, duller questions. In his thirty years of teaching in the New York City public school system, he told us, he'd found this system incomparably effective. They made SSA cards for nearly every subject, and he didn't understand why more teachers didn't use them. If they'd made them for lunch and gym, he would've recommended those too.

Mr. Flag had Melody pass out the SSA cards and the school-owned *History of the World* textbook. I stared out the window, past the schoolyard, toward the subway. I wished I was back in bed reading *Anne of the Island*. Melody paused at my desk and told me we were still on Unit Five. I'd missed the second half of World War I, and now we were on World War II. She said I hadn't missed much.

As the class set to work on the current SSA card, Mr. Flag called me to his desk and handed me the stack of cards I'd missed. On the subway that morning, I'd worried that some teacher might single me out and make an embarrassing show of sympathy. Mr. Flag's distant, pained smile and his lack of mentioning anything about my mother's death, as if I'd been out with a cold, seemed worse. I sank back into my seat and stared blankly at the SSA cards in front of me.

I watched Melody return to her desk and dutifully scrawl out the answers to every dry question, like the rest of the class. I stared back out the window. Suddenly I heard Mr. Flag's voice. "Are you having a problem with the assignment, Miss Pearlman?"

I shook my head.

"Then you should be writing."

I opened the book. *History of the World* was color-coded to go with the SSA cards. World War I was canary yellow, World War II a sky blue. I glanced over the long, thick, dry passages on governments, battle sites, statistics of lives lost. I turned the pages to look at the pictures. Red and yellow maps of countries' borders before and after the war. FDR in his wheelchair. A military army plane over the Pacific. Hitler at a podium, his moustache like a mistaken flick of a Magic Marker, a German banner waving behind him. Then, in the bottom right corner of the next page, the last photograph of the section: a concentration camp. Bodies, bone-thin, huddled, half alive, limbs strewn about so that you could not tell which belonged to whom. Then the chapter ended. The following page was electric orange, the beginning of Unit Six.

Everyone scribbled the assignment.

I stared at the page with its sky-blue border, the black-and-white photograph. I'd seen dozens of pictures and movies about the Holocaust and the camps before, of course. I'd read *The Diary of Anne Frank* and watched Holocaust movies-of-the-week on TV despite my mother's disdain. She never watched them. I was curious, and guilty for being curious. The books and movies never satisfied the curiosity; they never seemed real. Did Anne Frank mean it when she wrote that people were good at heart? Did she feel that after her family had been found, after she'd been taken to Bergen-Belsen?

My mother had met Anne's father, Otto Frank. He'd been friends with the Gluckmans, Fanny's parents, and my mother had been invited to dinner several times when Otto Frank was there. My mother was about ten years old. What was he like? I asked her, proud and envious. She shrugged. She said he seemed nice. It was before the diary had been published. She said he was thin and quiet, like everybody else.

I kept staring at the photograph. The silence of my mother's life became even greater right then, as I looked at the picture. She'd rarely spoken of what happened to her family during the war; she'd tried to shelter us from it. She'd wanted being Jewish just to be the songs for us, the food, but it couldn't be—those couldn't be separated from everything else. Her sheltering, her silence, had told us something darker just the same. My back prickled, my face grew hot. I stopped seeing the picture in the book and instead saw my family: my grandparents' eyes when they gazed at my sister and me playing, as if they'd never seen children do that before. My mother, digging her fingernails into my shoulder when she heard German spoken on the bus. Jamming her tote bag full of food and supplies, to be prepared "for anything." Calling the police after hearing fireworks one August night, waking my sister and me, thinking New York was being bombed.

This tiny photograph in the book, with no names, no explanations, no descriptions of who the bodies were, how they got there, if their families survived—this one chapter with its color-coded sections and corresponding questions—wasn't what my family had experienced. This book was about a one-event history, the kind of disaster that begins and ends, with no aftereffects, no reverberations. Not the kind of history that seeps in slowly and colors everything, like a quiet, daily kind of war, the war that my mother and my family lived through, which lived through them, which never ended.

I thought about my mother in the hospital, telling me that she'd always known this would happen, that she would die like this, that all her life she'd been waiting. Even that night of the diagnosis, behind the surprised smile had been something else: a knowing, an expecting.

And the shock was that hints of this had been dropped all my life–hadn't I read *Anne of Green Gables* and *Oliver Twist* for the first time, long before the diagnosis, with the same hunger with which I read them now? We'd only known my mom had cancer for twelve days, but the doctors said it could've been growing in her, undetected, for over twenty years. I wondered if that was the cause behind her years of vaguely identified allergies, asthma, colds; her days in bed; the darkness of her room, of every room in our house; her face buried in her hands; the crook of her elbow shielding her eyes. She had kept piles and piles of lists, reminding herself to do everything in a frantic, uneven script. We had repeated "I love you" to each other daily, incessantly, because my worst fear had always been that I would come home one day and find out she'd died, and she wouldn't know how much I loved her. We said it so often, I used to be afraid that someone outside of my family would catch my mother and me in a desperate "I love you"–or that I might accidentally say one to someone else. I'd even considered it superstitious–but it wasn't, I could see now. It was that I sensed, even then, how fragile and uncertain my mother's life was. That the hole her death left had begun forming a long, long time ago.

I stared out the barred windows to the cement schoolyard. I hadn't answered one question, not only on this card but on any in the stack. I hadn't even faked it, writing notes to friends like others did. My stark white notebook lay wide open, my pencil across the blank page.

The classroom was quiet. Mr. Flag watched me with a starched smile. "Miss Pearlman, if you're having problems with the blue section, you can go back and work on the yellow."

I couldn't turn the page. I sat frozen in my seat, transfixed by the picture; I couldn't look forward or backward or do anything but stay there, staring at the bodies, unknown, intertwined, tossing, their bodies, my mother's body, me.

A bell rang, the end of the period. Books slapped shut, assignments passed forward, notebook paper tore. I didn't move. I kept looking at the picture, and it seemed to me that the worst thing that could happen in the world right then would be to send my book forward like everyone else and pretend that it was just a photo in a book, in World History, Unit Five, and nothing else. As if the war was the kind of thing you could print in a color-coded textbook, shut at the end of the lesson, and give back.

Melody stood at the front of each row to collect the assignments and textbooks. I heard them flapping around me, moving forward.

Mr. Flag stared at me, impatient. "Miss Pearlman, are you going to pass your book in?"

The books lay in a neat stack on the first desk of our row, and Melody moved them into a pile on the windowsill. I couldn't move.

"Miss Pearlman, pass your book in, please."

He whispered something to Melody, and her patent leather Mary Janes clicked on the floor. I didn't know what I was going to do. I picked the book up. It felt surprisingly light in my hands. As Melody walked toward me, with Mr. Flag's stark face behind her, his fingers bent stiffly over his pink and white Delaney card system, each card filed into its neat compartment without a thought as to who existed in each one, his face with its expression of perpetual annoyance, like we were an incurable breed of disorder, disruption, and lost causes, the last thing I could do was place that book in Melody's hand. She was smiling, the same smile she'd had when she handed me the grief book, the five distinct stages I hadn't entered or passed and, it seemed now, never would.

She was still smiling when I threw the book at the window. The window was open, and it hit the metal bars with a loud clang, then clapped on top of the sill as the pages flurried open. The class flinched all at once. Mr. Flag did too, and though his features reassumed their rigid position and his face admitted hardly a change, the sound continued to ring in the silent classroom afterward.

Hospital Food

It seems to me that our three basic needs, for food and security and love, are so mixed and mingled and entwined that we cannot straightly think of one without the others.

—M.F.K. Fisher
The Gastronomical Me

WHEN MY MIDTERM grades arrived, I considered various ways to shield them from my father: *Oh, there are no grades this year,* I could say, or *U does not mean unsatisfactory, it means ultraperfect.* Or else I could spill ketchup on strategic spots. I'd stopped going to history class altogether in favor of sleeping late, and I often slept through my second-period English class as well. But it turned out that the report card didn't matter after all—that night, my father had a heart attack.

"It's probably nothing, just too many baked beans at dinner," was how he'd initially described his chest pains as our taxi careened over the 59th Street Bridge and on to New York University Medical Center. It was April, three months after my mother died; a freak snowstorm had hit the city a few days before, and its slushy gray remains still lurked on the corners. Within hours we learned he would have to stay in the hospital for monitoring and tests, and in a week would undergo triple bypass. It was his second heart attack; his first had been when he was thirty-five, before I was even born.

During those days before the bypass surgery, I lived off

ice cream. It was the only appealing thing in the hospital cafeteria. I wasn't the only one who ate it–I recognized the other visitors from the fifteenth floor, all of us standing beside the soft-serve machine, Styrofoam bowls extended, globbing on fudge, sprinkles, and whipped cream in some speechless camaraderie. Nobody cried openly in the hospital; we just stuffed our misery behind magazines, rumpled newspapers, and meals of dessert. I buried myself behind *Cardiovascular Surgery and Your Family,* the blue pamphlet the doctors had given us, and tried to convince myself that my father would be all right.

Doctors, relatives, and friends assured Alex and me that he'd be fine–bypass surgery was so common now that it was practically routine, they said–but each night I'd watch my sundae dissolve, not wanting to return to his room, to the tubes flowing from his body like plastic vines, the heart monitor exposing every wobbly beat, the electric clamps poised against the wall like a pair of praying hands. *A common procedure,* I'd repeat to myself, and then wallow in a melted pool of cookies 'n' cream.

I was sitting in a far corner of the cafeteria three days before the surgery when one of my father's doctors, an intern, approached me. "Can I join you?" he asked.

I nodded. I'd seen him dozens of times in the past week, whenever the team of doctors came into my father's room on their three-minute rounds, all of them inspecting my father's body and rattling off medical terms like a secret code. We'd never spoken. None of the doctors ever spoke to Alex and me; they glanced in our direction and smiled warily, as if we were the unfortunate audience of an unrehearsed show.

He introduced himself and we shook hands. I stared at his ID tag, like the kind factory workers wore: Richard E. Bridgewald. His face looked small and young in the little photo, overwhelmed by the white plastic around it. I searched his white coat for some sign of personality, some clue as to who he was—a monogrammed pen in his shirt pocket, a distinctive watch, a ring—but there was nothing.

Richard unloaded a salad, sandwich, and a glass of orange juice from his tray. "Where's your family?" he asked.

Family seemed an overly optimistic term for Alex, my father, and me. Most recently, Alex and I'd argued over which subway stop was closest to our house; that morning we'd huffed off to the 46th Street and 52nd Street stations separately.

"My sister's upstairs with our father," I said. I didn't know if I should mention that our mother was dead. I still wasn't used to saying the word *dead* out loud. I felt half disgusted and half fascinated by the word, as if it was a new, forbidden curse: *dead,* the real and unreal sound of it, absorbing and repelling, like a horror movie. *Night of the Living Dead. The Dead Return.* My father used the euphemisms—*she's gone, she passed away*—which, my sister pointed out with her usual delicacy, sounded like his *Excuse me, I just passed wind.* "Say *fart,* Dad," she'd demand.

"My mother died here—in this hospital—in January."

Richard rearranged his lettuce leaves. "I know—it's on your father's record. I'm sorry. "

I nodded, surprised. What else did he know about me? I pictured the doctors whispering about us in the back halls, the staff elevator: *The Pearlman daughters, they're regulars here.* I often stared at the doctors, settled in their roped-off section like a flock

49

of tired geese; I imagined mini-plots secretly unfolding among them, like on hospital TV shows. Sometimes I even peeked into staff lounges and restricted rooms, hoping to see doctors and nurses getting it on, orderlies in a fistfight, or patients screaming bloody murder. But nobody kissed, and no one fought. Even the emergency room, where my father had been that first night, had seemed surprisingly sedate: a kid with a button stuck up his nose, and lots of sleeping old people.

Why had Richard sat down with me? There were other families of his patients in the cafeteria. I studied his face. From time to time he glanced at me, between swallows, and there was an expression in his eyes I'd seen before—sad, almost regretful. It was how my mother's oncologist had gazed at us when he told us there was nothing more he could do for her. My sister had started sobbing while I'd stared at him blankly, stupidly. He'd wrapped an arm around my sister's shoulders; it looked strange, the sudden touching, mistaken and accidental, like a dancer falling.

I put down my spoon. "My dad's dying, isn't he?"

"No." He laughed nervously. "No. I didn't mean for you to think that. It's just—you looked worried here, all alone."

"I'm not worried," I lied, stirring my dissolving whipped cream.

"I was thinking, maybe with someone to talk to you probably wouldn't be so anxious about it all."

At first I thought by "someone to talk to" he meant himself, but he went on, "We have a great social work staff. Usually they talk to the patient and family when the case is terminal, but I was thinking because of your mother, we could have someone talk to you and your sister."

I thought of the social worker assigned to us while my mother was dying; he'd taken notes while she vomited in the bathroom. "I don't think–"

"It could be a real help. To you and your father. Usually families don't realize the kind of power they can have." He gently prodded a tomato with his fork. "Although your father's already lucky, with a daughter like you. Seems like you're at the hospital every night."

I wondered if he knew I spent more time leafing through the Harlequin Romances in the gift shop than in my father's room.

"He's lucky to have you," he repeated, smiling.

Suddenly, I knew why he'd sat down with me: in the last couple of months I'd been looking much older than I usually did. Yesterday a businessman had handed me his card on the 7 train, trying to pick me up; the cashier at the corner deli had asked where I went to college; a nurse had mistaken me to be older than Alex. My expanded morning routine was paying off–I'd been spending nearly two hours getting ready each day. I'd settle in front of my mother's lighted Clairol makeup mirror and curl my hair with her Style Pro. I applied her Estée Lauder Nude Mood eye shadow and Cool as Coral lipstick. I wallowed through her closets, plunging my hands into the silk shirts, sniffing the wools that still held her smell. Some of her clothes still had the tags on; I clipped them off and wore them. My father and sister hadn't noticed, and I was thankful–I didn't think they'd be pleased. After we'd picked out a dress for the burial my father had shut her closet doors with a certain finality, like closing a shrine.

"After you talk to the social worker, we can meet here so you can tell me how it went," Richard said. "Do you usually eat at this time?"

"Yes." I felt a sweet sort of chill. How old could Richard be? Twenty-six? Twenty-seven? It wasn't so much: my friend Lucy's parents had been nine years apart, my grandparents fifteen. And lately age had begun to seem like a vague, immeasurable thing, like when I saw Mrs. Kopecki, our neighbor who lived in a basement apartment across the street, for the first time after my mom had died. *I've never lost someone close to me, I can't imagine,* Mrs. Kopecki had said, suddenly distant and quiet. *Oh, you manage, you do,* I'd said, comforting her.

"What do you think? Should I arrange it?" he asked.

I nodded. It wasn't faith in the social worker that made me agree, but the knowledge that this would be a repeated thing, this shared meal. I ate breakfast alone on the subway platform and had stopped bringing my lunch to school; I bought cookies and Munchos at the snack truck across the street instead. Alex and I rarely ate together; she refused to even enter the hospital cafeteria, preferring to bring her beloved Turkish meat and spinach pies from the Turkiyem store near our house and gnaw on them in the solarium. But what a difference it made to eat leisurely, pleasantly, with somebody new—the clinking of their fork, their happy munching, the questions and glances, the whole fact of them beside you. When Richard and I finished and placed our trays on the conveyor belt, for the first time in weeks I felt full.

꒰꒦꒱

"I feel good," my father told Gina Petrollo, the social worker. "I feel great. I'll live till I'm eighty–another fifty-five years." He grinned at his own joke.

Gina laughed, her red nails clicking on the windowsill. Alex and I couldn't stop staring at her. Her butt mushroomed out of her white suit like a detachable cushion; her hair sprayed in black whirls from her barrette. She spoke with a Long Island accent, like the girls with teased hair and gold jewelry we saw in the dressing rooms of Filene's Basement, fighting over discounted panty hose. Richard had told me, when he'd come by with the team of doctors earlier that afternoon, that the woman assigned to us was known as the best on the staff. *You can tell me how it went at dinner tonight,* he'd said, and all afternoon I'd been cradling the thought of dinner, like a secret. While I pretended to do my biology homework, I'd scrawled *Richard Bridgewald* in different handwritings in the margins of my notebook. I added up the letters in our names to see if we were eternally fated to be together. It worked out.

Alex leaned toward me and whispered, "She wears even more makeup than you do."

"Her butt's even bigger than yours," I said.

"Up yours."

"Up *yours.*"

"Girls," my father warned, "I can't hear Miss Petrollo speak. And you're disturbing Mr. Grossman." Morty Grossman was the nearly comatose man in the next bed whom my father had befriended. He befriended everyone in the hospital, as if it was a big social club. *It's better than the Howard Johnson's here,* he'd said. *I get my TV, my Times, my Sanka, the river view.* And now he was offering Gina some coffee, like she was a guest in our home.

"The girls are always like this, kvetching," he told Gina. "But they're smart kids—my older daughter here, she's the mathematician and scientist. She won the Westinghouse science competition."

"Dad," Alex groaned.

He grinned at me. "The younger daughter wrote a book that's in the school library."

"That was, like, fourth grade," I said, staring down at the floor, wondering why he always had to refer to us in the third person.

"What a great book. What was it called?" He looked toward me, but I pretended I didn't remember.

"Smelly the Blue Sock, Superdetective," Alex volunteered.

"A great book," he reassured Gina.

I shook my head. He was acting so differently than he had when my mother was in the hospital. She'd put off the chemo three days, though the doctors told her it was her only chance; when my father and the doctors pressured her into doing it, she grew even sicker—she threw up, stopped eating, was barely conscious enough to speak until she died. *She's handling it all wrong,* our father had said to Alex and me when our mother wanted to stop taking the chemo. *She's weak. She can't cope.* The words still echoed in me, rolling into a tangled ball of anger, but I couldn't stay angry at him. Even before he went into the hospital, whenever I'd tried to be mad at him he'd suddenly say or do something unbearably loving, like when he explained why he'd been coming home so late after work: *I've been stopping by the cemetery to talk to Mommy,* he'd said. *To tell her about you girls, and the shop.* He'd said it so deadpan, so matter-of-factly, in his quiet, plain way, that his love for us stunned me, it was so constant and overwhelming.

Gina turned to Alex and me. "Why don't we talk in the solarium, so we can let your father and Mr. Grossman get some rest?" She spoke slowly, like she was teaching new vocabulary on *Sesame Street.*

We followed her butt to the solarium. I stared at the non-descript paintings on the walls, the wispy pastels. In the far corner a man snored on the leather couch; a woman in a wheelchair gaped out the window.

"You have such a nice family," Gina said.

We shrugged.

She scrawled something on her clipboard, as if we'd already answered wrong. "How do you feel about your father's surgery?"

Alex and I gazed at each other. "Okay," Alex said. "I mean, he's going to be all right, isn't he? That's what everyone keeps saying. We shouldn't be upset, right?"

"No, you shouldn't be," Gina said, smiling like a Crest ad. "Have you been feeling upset, Mia?"

I wasn't sure how to answer. I was embarrassed by the worries I had—as if they were paranoid or pessimistic. The hospital was like a perpetual purgatory, a holding place where all doubts and questions were frozen off, sucked into the sterilized, cotton-ball walls. It was as if no one wanted to admit that people actually died here. Everyone had been optimistic at first with my mother, too.

I stared down at the glossy white of Gina Petrollo's shoes until Alex answered for me.

"Mia's upset," Alex said. "She's failing her history class–"

"No, I'm not." How had she found out? I thought I'd successfully hidden my midterm report card.

She rolled her eyes. "She's not taking care of herself–she leaves late for school every morning and eats the most disgusting things." She poked me. "I mean, you don't even have breakfast, do you?" She turned back to Gina. "I think she has, like, Twinkies on the subway."

"That's not true," I said, wondering how she knew.

"Erratic eating is a common symptom of anxiety," Gina said, pleased with her diagnosis. "What you can do"–she reached into her handbag and pulled out another blue pamphlet, *Convalescence and Your Family*–"is read this through so you'll feel prepared to help your father recover. I think he's going to do wonderfully. He has a great attitude. He is so *strong*. And in the meantime, what you need to do to take care of him is to take care of yourself." She slid the new pamphlet toward me on the coffee table.

"I keep telling her he's going to be okay," Alex said, "but she doesn't believe me."

"For God's sake, they're sawing through his *chest*," I said. "They're rearranging his *heart*." I paused and stared at the pamphlet on the table. *Convalescence*. It sounded like the name of a perfume. "Everyone said Mommy was going to be fine at first," I added quietly.

My sister glared at me. I watched her fist come at me in slow motion, like they do in boxing movies. She punched me on the shoulder–not hard, but I toppled off my chair and gripped the table. A year ago, when Alex was studying behavior modification techniques in a psychology class and briefly decided to stop cursing, she'd taken to hitting me whenever I swore. I never hit her back, since she was bigger and stronger than me, but I screamed enough to make up for it.

"Fuck you!" I screeched. "You *goddamn* bitch!"

Gina's eyes widened like those of a farmer wandering upon fertile land.

Alex started crying. "That isn't the only thing," she told Gina, her voice quavering. "I see her every day–she's wearing Mommy's *clothes*." Her mouth twisted and widened as she sobbed, and she stormed off toward our father's room.

I gazed down at the floor guiltily. "Well," I said. Gina stared at me, as if awaiting some explanation. "You know, I should probably get back to my dad," I said.

She smiled gently. "We can continue our discussion later."

"That's okay. We don't have to."

Gina thoughtfully raised her plucked brows, as if struck by a sudden insight. "I know what you need." She rummaged through her pocketbook. I thought she was going to pull out another pamphlet–I hoped for *Romancing Doctors and Your Family*–but instead she handed me a tiny street map. "Macy's is right down Thirty-fourth Street. You walk fifteen minutes, you buy yourself some nice thing, you come back, and you'll feel so much better. You just need to get out of here. No one should be in the hospital this much."

I gawked at her. Where had she gotten her social work degree–Wilfred Beauty Academy? She patted my shoulder, said good-bye, and clicked off toward the elevator. In the solarium, the man still snored; the woman still wordlessly gaped out the window.

I didn't go to Macy's or return to my father's room right off; I took the elevator to the seventeenth floor, the cancer floor, and walked down to the public ladies' room, tucked away at the far end of the corridor. It was empty, as it had always been in January. It was the only place in the hospital where you could be alone.

I stared at myself in the mirror. I washed my hands with the disinfectant soap and dried them. They smelled like Lysol. I took out my mother's blusher and reapplied it. This bathroom was virtually the only place I'd cried while my mother was dying. I never did it in front of her, with the doctors and nurses coming in and out. Crying felt like failure, like admitting we'd lost; it was breaking the hospital's unwritten code, the hopeful façade that we were supposed to maintain.

The doctors had never sat us down and explained to us exactly what was going on with my mother; we were told of the dwindling prognosis only during quick exchanges in the hall. The day of the diagnosis, a Monday, she'd been given a good chance of remission; the next day she was given five years. Day by day the outlook worsened: on Saturday they said she might live two years, on Sunday one year, on Monday months, and then weeks. On Wednesday the gastroenterologist said to me in the hall in passing, throwing his hands up in the air, "Your mother comes in with a stomachache and finds out she's a dying woman!" He sounded exasperated with her, as if she'd somehow been deceptive, thoughtless, and unfair to hide such a grave state with so forgettable a symptom.

The following Saturday she'd fallen into a coma, and in the late afternoon, while my father, my sister, and I were in her hospital room, my mother stopped breathing. I had been watching her mouth opening and closing, and suddenly it stopped.

There'd been no chance to say good-bye like there is in the movies, no tearful resolutions and shared confessions. My sister moaned and screamed and hollered. I stood frozen, completely stunned; I didn't cry. The nurses came in, and then an orderly arrived; they asked us to take her jewelry off. I slid her rings onto my fingers, held her hand, which was already cold. I kissed her forehead. They wheeled her out. That was the last time I saw my mother.

And now I was wearing her maroon sweater, her print scarf. I couldn't keep away from her closets, the mysterious treasure trove of my mother. Each time I creaked open the huge wooden doors my stomach still clenched, as it had when we'd picked out a dress to bury her in. The closet had loomed before us, overflowing, shelves sagging, dress racks packed tight. Beautiful, expensive dresses towered out; twenty unopened packages of panty hose, stacks of belts, scarves, pants with the tags still on. We'd flinched in surprise—we'd known she'd bought lots of things, but it had never seemed this much, and we stood mesmerized by these clothes without their owner, like shed skins, discarded cocoons. The sheer amount even overwhelmed the usual criticisms parading from my father's and sister's mouths about our mother's spending habits. *Why?* Alex would ask when mail-order packages clogged the doorway, or our mother came home from work loaded down with shopping bags. *Why does she buy so much stuff?* My father would shrug and say, *Your mother had hardly any clothes as a child,* or some similar mystifying statement. Were our grandparents nudists? Could they not stand the fashions? *Omi and Opa came here with one suitcase* was my father's explanation. I thought of the unfamiliar names of the dead relatives on my sister's family tree–Friedl, Julius, Lotte, Gadi–and the question marks.

A tear slid from my eye. It was strange to watch it, as though it was somebody else's face, the eyes reddening, squinting. I had done it so often now I was a quiet-crying pro; I could do it without sobbing, without noises or heaving, just the tears flowing as if they were apart from the rest of me.

"I just spoke with Miss Petrollo," Richard told me at the salad bar that night. "She said she enjoyed your talk. She really likes you and your sister."

"I bet she does."

We set our trays down at the same table we'd eaten at before. Though I'd gazed longingly at the sundae station, I hadn't indulged; it seemed too childish beside him.

I stared down at my carrot shavings. I'd read magazine articles about how to tell if a guy liked you. *His pupils will dilate. He'll smile a lot and may even stutter. He'll stare at his feet. He might pinch or tickle you. He may act like a jerk.*

"She had a suggestion. She thinks it would be good if you could see your father after the surgery, on the sixth floor. He'll still be under the anesthetic then, but you'll be able to see he's fine."

The sixth floor: in the elevator, a little white cube with red lettering encircled that number, warning No Visitors Allowed. I doubted that any suggestion of Gina Petrollo's could possibly bring any good, and was about to tell Richard that we could just wait to see my father when he was awake, but Richard kept talking.

"I know it isn't much of a help, but I'm glad I've had this chance to at least try to make things easier in some way. You've only spoken to Miss Petrollo once and already you seem relieved."

"Oh, yeah," I said, slicing my lettuce into bite-size pieces. I didn't tell him that the relief was because of him.

After we finished eating and placed our salad bowls on the conveyor belt, I returned to my father's room. The heart monitor still broadcast every rhythm, and my sister hardly looked up from her *Quantum Mechanics III,* but the thought of Richard made it all affect me less, somehow. Part of me knew that it was unrealistic to hope for something, to transform our brief meeting into some whirlwind of eternal devotion. A tiny memory of Jay Kasper's pity date also poked through–but I still couldn't help hoping. I wasn't sure what I'd do if I didn't have Richard to think about. Even if it was unrealistic for us to be together now, what was to stop us from connecting in the future, like the characters in a romance novel, meeting on page two and again on page two hundred? I could see Richard and myself at more appropriate ages . . . me, having graduated from college, in a job (anything but social worker), until some minor incident–a friend's baby, a sprained wrist–took me to the hospital. Years would have passed–no matter. He'd have been through girlfriends, many of them, but never married. In hours, it would happen as we'd always known it would: we'd kiss outside the hospital, a deep, shocking kiss, and the other doctors, the passengers in traffic, the visitors, the social workers–the whole world–would stop and stare in surprise.

Alex still wasn't speaking to me the day of the surgery; she sat curled up in her square orange seat in the hospital lobby, with her calculator and protractor and textbook. I wandered in and out of the gift shop, carrying my books from school yet not opening one of them. I bought a new romance novel, *Rosamunde's Revelation,* and skipped to the sex scenes. I was hyper-awake from exhaustion; all night I'd been unable to sleep. At three o'clock I'd gotten out of bed and started watching television, flipping between reruns of *Twilight Zone* and *Love Boat,* and periodically visiting the kitchen to rummage through the freezer. I opened a yellow Tupperware container and found the frozen three-month-old carcass of Jay Kasper's Cocoa Krispies treats. Whenever I saw him in the halls at school now, he smiled at me faintly, as if he barely remembered who I was, and walked on. I threw his creation out and settled on a more recently purchased Sara Lee chocolate cake; I ate it frozen from the box while my imagination leaped and bounded off, alternating between scenes of my father on the operating table and visions of the wedding dress I'd marry Richard in, ivory sleeveless with long silk gloves.

At six that morning I'd started getting dressed. I didn't wear my mother's clothes, to try to keep peace with Alex for at least one day, but I used every kind of makeup my mother owned: eyebrow pencil and cheekbone highlighter, even a set of false eyelashes she'd bought for a Cleopatra costume one Halloween. I wore my own small wool hat and matching dress; in a moment of inspiration I stuffed my bra with cotton.

Late in the afternoon, I plopped down in the chair beside my sister, who was scribbling away in her notebook. For the first time that day she really looked at me.

"What's on your face?"

"Nothing."

She squinted. "Your eyes. They look weird."

"They're fake," I said, and blinked at her. "The eyelashes. They make my eyes look big."

She shook her head and went back to her work, and I read until I fell asleep. At five o'clock she nudged me awake–Richard stood before us in the lobby.

He looked tired but relieved. "It was a success," he said. "Everything went well. He's still unconscious–he will be for a while–but he looks good. I can take you up to see him."

We packed up our books and followed Richard to the staff elevator. We didn't speak. The tension of the past days and weeks trailed us into the elevator and up to the sixth floor.

No paintings hung on the walls of that floor; there were no couches, no solariums. Just random medical machinery I'd never seen before, parked throughout the corridors; the hulking machines looked like creatures from the future, as if they could scuttle away on their own. Nurses and doctors flurried by, their gazes gliding over our heads. Richard led us into the brightly lit recovery room. The beds were lined up like in an orphanage. He pointed out my father's body.

His bed was at my chest level. Alex and I stood stunned before it, hypnotized. The transparent blue of the oxygen mask, the clicking and whirring of pumps and electronics, the breathing machine, the closed eyes, the random spots of dried blood, brown on the blank bedsheet. My father's blood. It ran in tubes, transported to and from another machine. His whole body seemed like a technological, digital thing, as if where the machines started and stopped couldn't be defined.

It wasn't our father. It was some replacement, a wax model, a plaster shell. Our real father was upstairs with his *Times* and Sanka. The body in front of us was a mistake, and we stood there blinking at it, and at the other sheet-covered shapes with their mechanical breaths and computerized heartbeats, until finally Richard tapped our shoulders and led us out.

None of us spoke in the elevator, but Richard seemed proud and eager, as if seeing our father had actually pacified us somehow, instead of making me feel like I'd just seen him dead.

I held on to the straps of my book bag. Richard led us to the place where we'd been sitting before. He stared over our heads and stood beside us, as if waiting for something. I wanted to speak to him, to tell him that it wasn't my father in that bed—to let him comfort me, wrap me in his arms and keep everything away—but I couldn't say it; I didn't even know how to begin.

Richard's eyes focused on something down the hall; I

turned to see what it was. I heard Gina Petrollo's shoes clicking toward us even before her figure came into view.

"How did it go?" she asked, out of breath.

"Wonderfully," he said. "No complications–everything's fine."

He stretched out his arms; his hand touched the edge of her back. It was the tiniest gesture, a flick. If I hadn't been replaying his every movement again and again in my mind over the past three days, I'd have missed it. But there was something unmistakable in the motion that was intimate and familiar, the way my sister and I would sometimes pick a bug off each other; it was a touch that indicates more.

"I'm so glad," Gina said, grinning at us. "We were so worried about you." She reached over and enveloped my sister in a tight, long hug. Then she hugged me.

For a second I thought I'd suffocate, and I wanted to wrench myself away. But gathered into the pillow of her marshmallowy chest, inhaling her perfume, I almost didn't want to be released. I couldn't remember when I'd last been hugged–really, tightly hugged. Once clutched to her body, it almost didn't matter who she was, until she let go.

She stood beside Richard, who smiled at us.

"Thanks, for everything," Alex said quietly.

I couldn't speak. Richard and Gina said "you're welcome" with a kind of finality to their voices, and Richard shook our hands as he said good-bye.

As they walked off down the hall I started to cry. It was the first time I'd cried openly in the hospital. My body shook, my hat fell off, and some of the cotton balls roamed toward the middle of my chest; my rouge ran, and the eyeliner, the fake eyelashes, the whole great mass of it smeared off until I must have looked like modern art, a twisted Picasso, features falling all over the place.

"Look, you're shedding," Alex said, and plucked a hairy blob of false eyelash off my cheek. She held it up, like a spider.

I couldn't stop crying. I knew it was the wrong time to cry publicly now, so late for my mother's death, so prematurely for my father's. What no one ever tells you is that people don't die all at once, but again and again in waves, before their deaths and after. And I wasn't just crying for watching Richard leave with Gina, or seeing my father's body, or the fight with my sister, or even my mother. It was everything, suddenly–every person and object and speck of existence in the world seemed as if it could be lost. I kept crying until my sister put her arms around me, my fallen eyelashes folded inside a crumpled tissue, and said, "Come on," and took me to the cafeteria to eat.

My Mother's First Love

I began then to think of time as having a shape, something you could see, like a series of liquid transparencies, one laid on top of another. You don't look back along time but down through it, like water. Sometimes this comes to the surface, sometimes that, sometimes nothing. Nothing goes away.

—Margaret Atwood
Cat's Eye

THAT SUMMER, I kept dreaming about the man who was my mother's first love. In the dream I followed him, detective-like, slinking through museums, coffee shops, libraries, subway trains, hoping he'd lead me to my mother. He strode like a movie star, confident and oblivious to the rest of the world; at dusk he wound his way through Central Park, down narrow paths along patches of forest to a small, secluded lake. There, drying off by the shore, stood my mother. She looked nothing like she had when I last saw her, with her hair matted against the hospital pillow and her belly bloated with growths. By the lake her black hair gleamed like velvet; her stomach looked taut and smooth. *At last you've found us,* she said, reaching for my hand. *I've been waiting.*

The dream had started in my summer English class, when Ms. Poletti asked us to write a story about true love.

Groans all around. Billy Marino sailed a spitball at the blackboard. "I don't *know* any love stories," whined Luisa Rodriguez. Eddie Silva muttered "Bullshit" through his gold teeth. Marisol Peters ignored the class altogether to doodle across her NO GUNS IN SCHOOL! bookmark–a gift we'd all received from the Board of Education. I stared out the barred windows to the rolling pavement of the Bronx. I was in summer school for history and English; the only spring-semester class I'd excelled in was hygiene.

"Love is beauty," Ms. Poletti sighed, off in her own reverie. We'd just finished reading Elizabeth Barrett Browning in class; Ms. Poletti had recited each stanza in a Britain-meets-Bronx accent, her flower-patterned dress dipping frightfully low as her bosom heaved. She was an anomaly at our school, flitting about like a robin, perching on our desks to impart to each of us seeds of hope. Rumors about her abounded: Luisa swore she'd seen Ms. Poletti adjusting her G-string in the girls' bathroom; Billy had spotted someone on the subway reading a romance novel by a Madame Poletti. In the cafeteria and on the walk to the D train after school we made fun of her, arching our eyebrows, shrilling our voices, but the consensus was that she was an improvement over Mr. Tortolano, the English teacher we'd had that spring. He had been fired in May after his membership in the North American Man-Boy Love Association had been confirmed. Everyone was passing now–that is, everyone but me.

Failing English again was a particularly remarkable achievement, considering that I was the only native English-speaker in the class. I wasn't a terrible writer; my subjects were the problem. For the how-you-overcame-your-deepest-loss assignment I'd written "Snuffy: Better Off Dead," about my departed overweight gerbil, who'd suffered a slow and painful demise after getting stuck in the Habitrail. Most recently, for the topic of great social and political import, I'd completed "Plaid Pants: Should

They Be Outlawed?" which had garnered a round of applause when I'd read it to the class, but received yet another U.

Ms. Poletti called me to her desk that day after class. She sat there like a magistrate escaped from Las Vegas, her sequined glasses slipping down her nose. "Miss Pearlman," she said, "are you familiar with the phrase 'Attitude is everything'?" She tapped a pink fingernail on my compositions. "There's a *tone* to these essays that's not suitable for the assignments. Good writing isn't about glibness. It's about *life*. Think Elizabeth Barrett Browning. Think 'How Do I Love Thee?'"

She smoothed the ruffled pages. "Now, this Snuffy piece–I see things to admire here. Clear language. Solid composition." She removed her glasses. "Yet you haven't let your readers *feel* your triumph over this loss. What was your *connection* to Snuffy? What did he *mean* to you?"

I shrugged. I didn't know how to explain myself. All I knew was that after school and the subway ride home, when I put my mother's old typewriter on the dining room table, listened to my sister talk on the phone about logarithms, and heard my father snore in front of the TV (he liked to keep it on even while he slept, for company), the last thing I could write was something serious.

She surveyed the index card I'd filled in the first day of class. Under *In your own words, why did you not succeed in English during the regular school year?* I'd written, *My mother died; my father had a heart attack.* It was strange to see it on the stark white card–name, address, Social Security number, grade-point average, dead mother, sick father, heading for the orphanage.

"I know that other things have been going on in your life," Ms. Poletti said. "But if you fulfill the assignment just *one time,* you'll pass this class. I don't think you want to stay in high school an extra year."

I said I didn't think so either.

She sighed. "You shouldn't have trouble with this. It should be a pleasure to write about love."

That night Alex gabbed on the phone about sine and cosine curves, and my father wheezed on the couch while zebras leaped across the TV screen. The narrator droned on about mating practices as I settled in front of my mother's Smith Corona. The first thing that came to mind was my parents.

True Love

On a cold, rainy night in March, over a year ago, Simon Pearlman gave his wife, Greta, their twentieth-wedding-anniversary present.

"Is it clothes?" Greta asked excitedly, clutching the huge box. "A case of wine? A crate of imported fruit?"

"Better," Simon said.

Greta ripped open the cardboard to reveal a glimpse of shiny red enamel.

"What is it? What is it?"

shouted the Pearlmans' two charming young daughters.

The packaging fell away to reveal—a fire extinguisher.

"It was on special at Sears," Simon said, taking the extinguisher from her, stroking it lovingly. "Should we test it?"

Alex, the elder daughter, jumped up excitedly. "Yes! Yes!" she cried. The younger daughter, Mia, shook her head like her mother; neither of them was very interested in fire extinguishers.

"Simon," Greta groaned, "we don't have time to test it. We're supposed to be at the restaurant *now*. You *agreed*, for *once*, to go out tonight."

Simon didn't hear her. "I think that hooks there," he mumbled to Alex.

"*Simon*, will you listen to me?" Greta screamed.

Simon didn't look up.

"For *once*, will you just *listen* to me?!"

"Just a second—"

"*Simon!*" Greta lifted a plastic

ashtray off the nearest shelf. She
threw it at him. It missed and
bounced off the floor. She picked
up a candle in the shape of a
turtle—a Chanukah present from her
daughters years ago.
  "Not the wax turtle!" the daughters shouted. "Not the wax turtle!"

I crumpled it up; this was not a love story. My parents had
fought so frequently that eventually Alex and I removed all
fragile objects from their shelves, and at night I'd lie awake listening to the arguing, my sheet wound in my fist as they
screamed. In the beginning Alex and I had tried, in little ways,
to repair our parents' marriage: we taped the praising *Queens
Independent* write-up of our father's shoe repair shop to the
refrigerator; we ordered two oversized laminated buttons
made from their wedding photo. But soon my mother began to
call her friend Fanny nearly every night (Fanny had divorced
her husband, Irv, four years earlier) and whisper on the phone.

Fanny told my mother to give up trying to drag my father
to restaurants and the ballet, and to take me instead. I loved
being my mother's date: together at Lincoln Center we'd cas-
cade past the outdoor fountain, through the main hall, past
the rustling taffeta and swishing silk of the finely dressed
ladies with their sweeping furs and wafts of expensive perfume. I pretended we lived there, in this mansiony hall with
marble banisters and chandeliers like explosions of glass.
Afterward we'd linger at the Pirouette Café across the street,

heavily under the spell of the performance, not ready to go home. Queens—my father and his stories of hammertoes and plantar warts, my sister shouting at her calculator as she practiced for Math Team—seemed like somebody else's life. For the first time, I began to wonder whether my parents should be married after all.

One night at the Pirouette last summer, seven months before my mother died, her mind seemed elsewhere. "I was talking to Fanny the other day," she said. "She invited me to come visit, for a little vacation. I was thinking you might like to come too, and see Lucy."

I'd been friends with Lucy Gluckman since I was three, when she and her parents lived four blocks away; I hadn't seen her since the divorce. In her letters she said she liked Maplewood, in upstate New York, much better: the houses weren't attached, as they were in Queens—no more crazy Mrs. Fonchette scratching on the walls. And her father arrived for visits with presents overflowing from the trunk. Her boyfriend, Brad, was captain of the lacrosse team; in ballet class she was now working *en pointe*. Not wanting to feel left behind, I'd embellished my own life: I invented a passionate affair with Luigi, the handsome clerk at Cardially Yours, our corner gift shop; I told her that my recital at the Flushing Academy of Dance had received a standing ovation, when in reality I'd pranced across the floor twelve counts early, like an escaped jumping bean. But the embellishments never seemed entirely false—sometimes at the Pirouette, after a performance, a part of me actually believed that one day I would be a dancer, twirling around that huge stage, leaping into Luigi's arms.

"You'd like Maplewood," my mother said. "There's shopping, forests and lakes, and the community center, where Fanny teaches folk dancing. You could even take ballet there if you wanted."

"It might be weird seeing Lucy—it's been so long," I said, wondering how I'd explain my less-than-stellar ballet technique.

"Maybe at first. Then things'll be like before. Some of the people in Maplewood I haven't seen in years—old friends from Washington Heights. People I've been wanting to see for a long time. Fanny said she's surprised how little they've changed."

Whenever we drove through Washington Heights my mother shuddered, remembering the grave-faced men and women shuffling from store to synagogue to their tiny, crumbling apartments, undecorated and bare—not like homes, my mother said. She told me once that her parents never hugged her; I couldn't even imagine it, our hugs were such an event. Even at fourteen I'd sit on her lap on the couch some nights, facing her, nuzzling my nose into her neck, talking as she kissed my hair—"huggies," we called these moments, like they were a game or a performance.

"Why'd your old friends move to Maplewood?" I asked.

She shrugged. "I guess to be happier. To get away. To find a better life."

Fanny and Lucy met us at the bus stop in a yellow Volkswagen Bug; Fanny lumbered toward us in her Birkenstocks. "Ya look gorgeous!" she told my mother.

"So do you!"

"That's what they tell me. I say leaving Irv took ten years off my age."

Lucy hugged me briskly. I didn't know what to say at first. "How's Brad?" I finally asked.

"Oh, good. You know. We're okay. And Luigi?"

"He's pretty good. Actually I haven't seen him much lately. He's really busy—selling those cards and all."

"Brad's busy too. You know—we kind of broke up."

"Really? Oh my God. I bet me and Luigi are going to break up too."

"It's really not that bad. My mother says I'm better off."

We stared at our mothers, giggling like teenagers in the front seat. They gossiped the whole drive, and all the way up the gravel road to the house. It was a gingerbread bungalow plopped in a sea of bright grass, the blades soft and cottony, whispering under my shoes.

"The block has a service that mows it," Fanny said. "Can you imagine if we had lawns in Queens? I'd have spent half my life getting Irv to mow."

My mother settled into the guest room while Lucy and I prepared the bottom half of her trundle bed. We dressed up for dinner at the Maplewood Grill: skirts and purses and high-heeled shoes. I gazed at the sky outside the restaurant, certain I'd never seen so many stars. We sprawled out in our cushiony booth; our mothers lit cigarettes and let us take sips of their wine.

"I'm so glad you're staying two whole weeks—a week from Saturday is Summer Showcase," Fanny said. "The whole town comes out. My class is performing first—four versions of the hora. I'm hoping the girls will dance too."

"*Ma,*" Lucy groaned, "not the *hora*."

"How are you going to get the boys to notice you if you don't shake your cute tush?"

"*Ma!*"

"These girls don't know how lucky they are–dinners out, dance classes. What did we have when we were their age? Boiled potatoes. Hopscotch. There was no music in our house. No dancing. No stomping around. No talking above a whisper. What did my father think–we'd be arrested by the Gestapo, lurking outside in New York?"

"Elsa became a dancer," my mother said. "Remember Elsa? Elsa Goldstone. I think she even made it to the Joffrey."

Fanny raised her eyebrows. "Then she danced her way out a sixth-story window. A little more graceful than Jack Cohen. You know, I ran into someone who knew his wife–said she came home one night, found him dead on the couch. Pills."

I stared at Lucy, frozen in her seat. We had always frozen whenever our mothers' conversation turned to people they'd known–survivors or children of survivors–who'd gone over the edge. The stories made me fear for my mother's life; it seemed suspended by a single thread. I couldn't make sense of her emotions: we had our nights out, the ballet, but then there were those hours she spent in bed, sleeping off an undefined illness. And there were the fights with my father, like sudden explosions, and her Wednesday-night trips to Dr. Mallik, her therapist, whom Fanny had recommended. Fanny shared many of my mother's quirks: the tote bags loaded with provisions, the way they kept track of Lucy and me, wanting intricate details of our plans at all times, as if once they lost track of us for a minute, they'd lose us forever.

And the way, when they said good night to us, they told us they loved us as if they doubted that we'd still be there in the morning.

Our hugs and food and declarations of love—I knew how much these gestures meant to my mother, and this knowledge gave me an odd kind of power: I knew that she'd never had this guaranteed love with anyone before, that her happiness seemed inextricably entwined with mine. But I depended on her too; I lived for her hugs, her food, and I told her I loved her with her same intensity, as if to say, *You have to live—if for nothing else, then for me.*

My mother's attention to me, though, seemed to lag after the first few days in Maplewood. In the mornings Fanny deposited me and Lucy at ballet class, while my mother slept in; I didn't see her until dinner. She seemed quiet and distant then, but peaceful, even satisfied.

"What'd you do all day?" I'd ask her at dinner.

"Oh, nothing—sit by the lake. Relax. Read some."

Fanny had given her a whole pile of books, including *Fear of Flying, Heartburn,* and *The Women's Room*; my mother pressed wildflowers between the pages. She was definitely enjoying life in this town, and I was too—the clean white sidewalks of Main Street, the wide, airy aisles of Stop & Shop, nights in bed beside Lucy, reading our Sweet Valley High books out loud. Even ballet was better than I'd expected. Lucy did wear toe shoes, but she kept tripping over them, and the instructor, Jolée, didn't even notice me twirling off count.

"Think how good we'd be if we danced together all the

time," Lucy said, nearly falling over from her arabesque. "We'd be like Baryshnikov and Gelsey Kirkland. Torvill and Dean without ice."

In Jolée's class we'd become a regular pair: each day, for our improvisation, we invented a two-minute ballet and performed it as a couple. It didn't matter what we looked like; Jolée simply crooned, "Feel the *mooovement,* become the *mooovement,*" and nodded in praise.

Out of the whole class, only one girl had mooovements that seemed on target, even beautiful, and Lucy and I often stopped to gape at her with envy. She was seventeen, with black hair that swept to her hips, and breasts that made ours seem like walnuts. Jolée adored her. It wasn't until late in the week that I found out her name: Greta, just like my mother's.

"Isn't that weird?" I said to my mother at dinner that night. "Isn't that the craziest coincidence? Another Greta. I never met anyone else with your name."

My mother shrugged; she didn't seem fazed or surprised, but Fanny kept smirking at me and then glanced at my mother and said, "Honey, it's not a coincidence–Greta's father was your mother's old boyfriend. He's a widower now."

I gazed at my mother. Sometimes she would tell me about the men she'd gone out with before she met my father: Moshe the Israeli; Charlie the Navy sailor, whose whole crew stood up when she entered the room; Harry the Californian, with the red convertible. I always felt envious and proud that my mother had had all these boyfriends, that she was so attractive and desirable, that she'd had this whole other exciting, romantic life, as I hoped I would someday.

"Greta's father's Moshe?" I said. "Or Harry with the sports car?"

My mother laughed. "No, no. This was the first boyfriend I ever had. Rolf–Rolf Stein."

Rolf. I peppered her with questions. She'd known him since she was my age, growing up in Washington Heights; unlike her family, who'd escaped to America at the beginning of the war, Rolf's had gone to Holland. His parents hid him in a Dutch orphanage, and he never heard from them again.

"We were engaged when I was eighteen," my mother said. "But before we could get married, he wanted some proof that his parents were actually dead. He'd had this hope, all those years, that they might still be alive. He left for Europe then–Germany, Holland, France, Russia. This long search. He found someone who'd known them in Amsterdam, someone who thought they'd been sent to Treblinka and survived."

He'd sent my mother postcards from across Europe for more than a year; suddenly the postcards stopped coming.

"What happened?" I asked. "What then?"

She shrugged. "Nothing. I married your father."

In bed that night, Lucy and I couldn't stop talking about it.

"Oh my God. It's so romantic. To name his daughter after your mother. He must have really loved her."

"I guess. I guess he did."

We recounted the story again and again. Drama, it was. Romance. *The Sound of Music,* starring my mother. In our minds Rolf grew as handsome and dashing as Christopher Plummer; my father became the balding understudy, with too-short corduroys and mismatched socks.

Lucy had seen Rolf only in passing; she couldn't remember what he looked like. "But I'm sure he's gorgeous. I bet you he'll be at Summer Showcase. Everybody goes. My God—we're really going to meet him."

As the showcase approached, Jolée told us that we could each perform a five-minute dance onstage. Lucy and I knew exactly what we'd do: we were going to dance the saga of my mother's first love. We choreographed it expertly. For the war we donned black leotards and galumphed across the stage; then we changed to purple and swept toward each other with elegance and grace; then we crumpled apart. We ended together in a passionate embrace.

As we rehearsed for Saturday, we decided that watching the dance would reunite my mother with her true love. She and Rolf would see the performance and recognize that their love had never ended; my mother would marry Rolf and we'd move to Maplewood; Fanny would marry Rolf's long-lost cousin, who'd suddenly appear, and Lucy and I would be related for real. We didn't even think of Lucy's father, my father, or my sister; in Maplewood the rest of the world seemed to disappear. It felt possible that everyone could be happy.

On the morning of the performance I woke up feeling sick, with a sharp, shooting pain around my stomach. I wasn't sure if the cause was anxiety or something concrete, but by the afternoon, at rehearsal, it hadn't gone away.

"I don't feel so well," I told Lucy.

"It's probably just nerves," she said. "You're scared of the responsibility. The pressure. It isn't easy, reuniting old loves."

I hugged my abdomen. "I don't know. Maybe–it could be my *friend*."

"Oh," Lucy said knowingly: my period. "Is she supposed to be visiting now?"

"She's early, I think."

"She really makes you sick?"

"Yeah. Kind of." I'd rarely told anyone, aside from my mother, how sick my period made me. For most eighth graders, cramps were the imaginary, convenient excuse for getting out of typing, math, or gym, but I was almost doubled over by the pains. I was embarrassed by how badly they affected me, how I missed school and threw up and ran fevers, spending all day in bed, writhing and crying, praying for the Midol to kick in. Even my father didn't wholly believe the pain was real; he seemed frightened of me then, averting his eyes when he asked me how I felt. And he wasn't unsympathetic just because he was a man–Alex didn't believe me either. We never confided our womanly secrets; when she first got her period, stealthily popping the Kotex into our shopping cart, I was shocked and elated, expectant and jealous. "What's it feel like?" I'd asked her, eager to share in the delights of her budding womanhood. "Shut the fuck up," she'd said.

My mother was the only one who believed the pain was real. To her, any illness, menstrual or not, became an occasion. Out came the ginger ale, strawberry Jell-O, soup; sometimes she'd stay home from work, and when the painkillers finally kicked in, we'd paint with watercolors and play board games I was far too old for. She brought up trays of food for me to eat in bed–sandwiches with the crusts cut off, saltines spread with peanut butter and jam.

But now, all day, as rain poured down outside, we'd been practicing, decorating, and preparing for the showcase; I wouldn't see my mother till it was over.

"Once we start dancing, you'll forget it hurts at all," Lucy told me. "You'll be fine."

But by evening my cramps were even worse. At six-thirty, half an hour before the performance, I pulled off my leotard in the bathroom.

Blood. Drips and gobs of it on my underwear; I recoiled at the sight. I always felt shocked and surprised at seeing the blood: the sudden horror of the redness, so frightfully bright. I never accepted that all this blood outside my body could actually be a normal thing.

I found Lucy backstage. "I'm *really* sick," I said. "My friend's *here*."

"Can't you just take care of it? No one will know." She

glanced out at the auditorium. "You have to go on. The dance–we can't not do the dance. I can't do it without you."

She summoned Jolée, who suggested I try deep breathing methods, and Fanny, who procured Midol from someone in her hora group.

"Do you know where my mother is?" I asked Fanny, my voice beginning to break. "I need to see her."

She looked around at the people filing into the auditorium. She seemed nervous. "I don't know. I haven't seen her since this morning. Maybe–she might be by the lake. But honey–" She reached her hand out to me, but I started running, past Fanny, Lucy, Jolée, out the stage doors. I didn't know what I was doing. The performance, our rehearsals, our plans to reunite my mother and Rolf–suddenly none of them mattered. I had to see my mother now; I had to know where she was. I wanted not just her comfort but the assurance of her presence. For a moment I felt like I was the mother, worried about her daughter's whereabouts, needing the fact of her life to validate mine.

The rain had stopped. I ran the whole way to the lake, half a mile, moisture from the grass soaking through my pink ballet slippers, mud splattering onto my tights. Near the lake I paused, panting. My mother, her back to me, was sitting quietly at the water's edge. A man sat beside her.

"Mom!" I called out. "Mom!"

She turned and stared at me, standing there sopping wet and streaked with mud; she looked at me as if I was crazy.

"I'm really sick. I think–I think I need to go home."

I didn't get a good look at Rolf. In the rush all I saw was the dark form of his body, shaded angles of his face. My memories after that are shady too, my brain trying to edit out my clumsiness, my humiliation at destroying my mother's love scene. I remember my mother taking me home to clean me up, and, later, apologies to Fanny for missing the performance, Lucy's silent disappointment, my mother's quick decision that we had better leave that night–that I'd probably feel better if I just got back to Queens.

On the bus ride home my mother showed no sympathy. I vomited in the bus bathroom; I sniffled in my seat. My mother hugged her pocketbook to her lap and gazed out the window, not listening. She seemed torn between Maplewood and Queens, angered by her decision, her obligation, to return home. I didn't know what had happened between her and Rolf; I couldn't ask. Midway through the ride a woman tripped over my bag in the aisle. "Stop being so goddamn careless!" my mother screamed at me.

I gathered my bag to my chest. A month before, the last time I'd gotten sick from my period, we'd missed a ballet performance because of it. My mother had said it didn't matter, and she'd told me what she really felt about dancing then. In reality it wasn't a life, she'd said. You couldn't see it on the dancers' faces, but underneath they were all in pain–bloody toes, torn ligaments. They were all hiding tremendous suffering.

I cried that night on the bus, noiselessly, my face turned toward the aisle, buried against the seat so that my mother wouldn't see. It was guilty crying, over my own selfishness. That dancers hid their suffering seemed noble; they endured pain for something beautiful. And I'd been unable to make that sacrifice, or even come close; self-absorbed, I'd embraced my pain, shouted it, flaunted it, as if it was something unique.

Little changed after we returned home: my parents' fights continued, my father still spent some nights on the couch, my mother murmured to Fanny on the phone. Lucy forgave me for missing the performance, and wanted me to come visit again. But my mother rarely mentioned our trip to Maplewood and never spoke of Rolf to me. I didn't bring it up. I was grateful that our relationship seemed the same as it always had been: hugs, evenings at the Pirouette, declarations of love.

Then one night, two months after we'd come home, my mother said good-bye to Fanny on the phone and passed the receiver to me. "You have to watch out for your mother—it's bad news," Fanny said. "Rolf . . . he passed away. I can't believe it. I just . . . I can't believe it at all."

"Passed away" seemed the wrong choice of words when she told me what had happened: Greta had come home after school one afternoon to find him hanging from an exposed rafter in an upstairs bedroom.

That night I went to my mother's room to try to comfort her. I brought up milk and crackers, arranged on a tray. But she lay asleep in the darkness, surrounded by her open notebooks. I shut the door and returned to my room.

I didn't know what to make of Rolf's death. In January, four months later, my mother was diagnosed. In the twelve days between the diagnosis and her death, Fanny sent packages of self-healing books: *Medicine and Miracles, Think Yourself Well.* When my father called Fanny to tell her my mom had died, I spoke to her afterward on the phone. She said, "It was your mother's depression. Really, it's not so different from Elsa or Jack. Or from Rolf. I've seen it happen to so many people. . . ." She trailed off and began to cry.

I didn't know what to say to her. Part of me wanted to scream at Fanny that my mother could not have brought it on herself. She could not have wanted to die.

But perhaps my mother hadn't brought it on herself; perhaps we were to blame—my father, my sister, and I—in our inability to give her what she wanted. What if that night in Maplewood, I'd said, *Stay with Rolf, Mommy! He's yours! You should be happy with your own life!*

I didn't say any of this to Fanny. I just said, "Uh-huh. I have to go now," and hung up the phone.

The sun began to come up. My father still slept on the couch. Outside, a garbage truck groaned down our street. Our neighbors' bed rattled against their side of the wall.

"True Love" was all I'd typed on the page during the night. At some point I'd fallen asleep across from my father, at the other end of the couch. I'd dreamed of Rolf and had trailed him to where my mother was, where she surely must be: in some other universe, alive and happy, with him.

For a few moments, in that hazy transition into waking life, a dream lingers as reality: Rolf's form strong and permanent, my mother lithe and healthy and satisfied. The peacefulness that surrounded them was what stayed with me the most in the seconds before I completely awoke–the rightness of it, of true love reunited. It seemed like the perfect ending to their story, a story Ms. Poletti might write, one she'd certainly approve of.

But I'd barely become accustomed to that picture when it began to evaporate. Outside, the garbage truck creaked, car horns honked, a taxi driver yelled. On the dining room shelf– the shelf my mother had once tossed objects off–lay one of the oversized buttons my sister and I had made of our parents' wedding photo. In that photo my mother smiled with the same satisfaction she'd shown in Maplewood. The same expression she'd had in the dream.

My father had said to me once, soon after he came home from the hospital, in the car driving over the bridge to Manhattan: "The problem with Mommy was that she never believed I loved her. I told her I did, but she never believed it was true."

At first I balked, not believing that any of my father's perceptions could be right. But of course he had loved her: his grief was as clear as mine since she'd been gone. And I thought about my mother, growing up without ever being hugged. Despite the lack of love she'd felt in her own life, she'd managed, somehow, to love me. The night we left Maplewood, after the long bus ride home, I awoke in the middle of the night to find a tray of ginger ale and sandwiches, the crusts cut off, and my mother next to my bed, her hand on my stomach, assuring me then and always that the pain was natural after all.

The Healthy Heart

*t*hat is the fearful part of having been near death. One knows how easy it is to die. The barriers that are up for everybody else are down for you, and you've only to slip through.

—Katherine Mansfield
The Letters of Katherine Mansfield

THE WORST THING I ever saw in the hospital was a birthday party. It was one of the nights that my father shared a room with three other men. Curtains were drawn, but you could easily peek past the orange and brown stripes to the other beds. In one corner, a few tufts of white hair curled out from a lump under the sheet; in another, a gray-bearded man gazed at his electronic heartbeat as if it was a lava lamp; and diagonally, in the fourth bed, a young guy had his nineteenth birthday party.

I'd seen this guy's party in April, soon after my father's bypass surgery; it was August now, but I still couldn't stop thinking about him.

His stubble-covered head had been shadowy with sprouts of longer, darker hair. He had friends, cake, and balloons around the bed, like a little kid's party. They couldn't light the candles because of the oxygen in the room, so he made a wish and pretended to blow out the nonexistent flames. His mother offered cake and soda to my sister and me.

"Thanks," we said, and she served a slice to each of us. It was a grocery store cake with yellow layers like a dish sponge and thick globs of icing that tasted like marshmallow and lard. I picked at it, thinking that I'd better eat it, considering.

His mother touched my elbow. "I'd like to find a doctor while I'm here," she said. "If you know what I mean." She had a thick Brooklyn accent and gesticulated as she talked, her gold bracelets jingling.

I thought of Richard Bridgewald and cringed. I tried not to stare at her son, but my eyes kept darting back to him.

Alex asked her, "Do you need a checkup?"

"He can do what he wants." She laughed. "See, if they know you, then you got it made. Then you can trust them. If you're married to one of them, you get the best service. My friend Patty, she has a cousin in Vegas who's married to a doctor and always gets a private room. It's about connections. Look here. If I was married to one of them, we'd be in a private."

I glanced at my father. He'd never had a private.

"You know, in street clothes, though, they're not so good-looking. I saw the oncologist, Dr. Kornovoy–I saw him on the corner of Thirty-fourth, and he had this green sweater on with these huge purple dots. You'd think with their kind of money he could buy a nice-looking sweater."

Her son, in the bed, rolled his eyes.

She introduced herself–her name was Gigi Backus–and her son, Sasha (a girl's name, I thought, though he didn't look girlish, even though he was thin and pale with blue eyes and jet-black lashes). Gigi's eyes were lined in smeared charcoal, her lips glistened with gloss, and her hair was whipped into a yellow froth. She looked too young to be his mother.

She lowered her voice. "They're flushing out his system."

I pictured a huge toilet with hoses or some hulking vacuum cleaner.

"Mom," the boy said. Gigi went over to him, and he whispered something in her ear.

I knew I should wish him a happy birthday, but I couldn't. A part of me wanted to be extra nice, and another part thought I should ignore him—he wouldn't want my charity. And what could I say? *Happy birthday!* says the healthy fifteen-year-old girl. *Many happy returns! Thanks for the yummy cake!*

I felt sort of sick from the whole thing, stunned by the whole soap opera traffic-accident scene of the young guy dying. But in a soap opera he'd get up at the end and walk away and live. If he died, it would be because he was a dispensable character, unimportant to the show.

When we left the hospital that night I told my sister, "I feel bad for him."

"Who?"

"That guy—Sasha."

"Who?"

"You know. The cancer guy."

"Oh. The cancer guy."

After that, we referred to him as the cancer guy. As in: *Be quiet, the cancer guy is sleeping.* And: *I saw the cancer guy in the hallway, he's looking better.* And in my diary: *I think the cancer guy is kind of cute.*

Now it was four months later, long after my father was home from the hospital, and I was still thinking of the cancer guy, wondering if he was still alive. He was in my mind even as we waited at the Port Authority bus terminal with my sister, who was about to leave for college. Our father was going on about having to give up smoked fish.

"Sable. Lox. Kippers. Sturgeon," he incanted, as if in a trance, as if reciting some kind of smoked-fish poem.

My sister rolled her eyes. She shifted her purple knapsack on her shoulder and stared down the dirty red-and-beige-tiled corridor.

"What about nova?" I asked him.

He shook his head. "Nova. Still too salty." The saltiness was the problem: he was prone to fluid in the lungs, which was aggravated by salt.

My sister took her knapsack off and stuffed her Curious George even deeper inside, though he didn't entirely fit and part of his head poked out. He'd been slept on so long he looked like he'd been stuck in a flower press.

She'd received a scholarship to Cornell and was leaving early for her orientation program. My father had wanted to drive her to Ithaca, but she preferred to take the bus.

The driver approached the line and started taking tickets. "Well, bye," my sister said, and hugged us quickly.

"You have the calling card?" my father asked.

"*Yes.*"

"Call when you get in," he said. She nodded and gave her ticket to the driver.

"Bye, Curious," I said to the ear sticking out of her knapsack.

"Bye," she said again. She walked to the bus, loaded her duffel bag into the luggage compartment, waved, and disappeared behind the tinted windows. Just like that, she was gone.

My dad said: "Well."

We kept standing in the corridor. "Let's wait till it takes off," he said. We moved to the uncomfortable swing-down bench (invented to stop homeless people from sleeping on it, my father declared) and waited. Neither of us mentioned my mother. She would have insisted on driving to Ithaca, I thought, or accompanying my sister there on the bus. She would have made her pack an extra duffel filled with brand-new towels and sheets. My father had told Alex to take her old Snoopy sheets with her; they were good enough.

Not that I could feel sorry for us anymore. Ever since seeing the cancer guy I'd felt guilty for mourning my mother because she had been so much older than him, decades older; compared to him she'd lived a long life. Who was I to complain over old Snoopy sheets?

The bus groaned, exhaled, and squealed off. When it was out of view we got up and headed toward 39th Street, where the car was parked.

The air felt heavy and strange now that my sister wasn't with us—it seemed as if all of New York had been rearranged. The streets looked unfamiliar and wrong. My father walked in front of me; he wore shorts in the August heat. Frankenstein-like scars ran down the insides of his legs, where they'd removed veins for his bypass surgery. The scars mortified me—why did he flash them for all to see? Most things about my father had begun to mortify me. He wore T-shirts splotched with coffee or mustard stains and didn't notice. He chewed with his mouth open.

He had bad teeth–horrible teeth that had been capped when he was little, and now the caps had worn through to rings of silver and gold and raw beige aging tooth.

"I wish you'd just wear pants," I said.

"It's hotter than hell out here. The street's melting." He got in the car and unlocked the passenger door, and I sat on the hot velour seat.

My father said, "I want you and me to go on a vacation."

"What?" The only vacations we'd ever taken as a family were to the Poconos; we'd rent a house for a week, swim in a lake all day, and stare up at the stars at night. My mind was deluged by disturbing images of my father and me alone in the Poconos, him trying to canoe in his Gilligan-style sun hat. Or, even worse, of us driving to the Grand Canyon in our ailing Mercury Zephyr, spending untold hours listening to his beloved Willie Nelson tapes. (Who could spend his whole life in New York City and love Willie Nelson?)

"I still have summer school," I said. "It's not over yet." I seemed to be passing my summer school classes, for which I was thankful. Ms. Poletti had actually approved of my final, completely fictional "True Love" story, which had featured a girl named Catherine and a tempestuous lad named Heathcliff and which took place on the hidden moors of Queens. I'd even woven in an Elizabeth Barrett Browning poem for good measure. She'd loved it.

"You only have three days left. We won't leave until next Sunday."

"I have a job. The Queens Burger needs me." I'd been waitressing there after school three nights a week.

"It's a diner–they don't *need* anyone. You can take a week off."

He took a return envelope from AT&T out of his shirt pocket; he liked to use garbage as his daily planner. "It's the Healthy Heart Week," he read off the torn flap, "hosted at the Green Springs Health Resort, sponsored by Virginia University Hospital. A companion is suggested for attendance. Also, it's underenrolled, so they dropped the price."

"I don't want to go to Virginia."

"You'll love it. They have a swimming pool."

"I can't swim!"

"You'll take a lesson." He tuned the radio to a country music station, to some man crooning about his bruised heart or burnt-down house or dead dog–I could never tell the difference. I pictured my sister's bus barreling up the highway to Ithaca. Where was Ithaca, anyway? She'd shown me on the map, and I couldn't even remember. It seemed so far away it could've been Nebraska or Idaho. It seemed even farther away than Virginia. I pictured the college's castle-like buildings and gorges, its campus paradise. "You're going to be living in the middle of a park," I'd told her.

She'd beamed. She couldn't believe it either.

At home, my father went about his business as if nothing had changed–he turned on the air conditioner and poured himself a glass of caffeine-free Coke. I wished I was the one on that bus.

"Look at this." He handed me the Green Springs brochure.

THE HEALTHY HEART WEEK
HEALING AND RENEWAL FOR THOSE
AT RISK AND THEIR FAMILIES

Heart disease is the number one killer of men and women. Are you or your loved ones at risk? Learn how to modify diet, stress, and exercise habits to increase your health, longevity, and happiness. Our program has three pillars: diet, stress reduction, and exercise. Take a cooking class, learn tennis or tai chi, and acquire the ability to relax even under the most stressful circumstances. Physicians will be on hand for personal evaluations.

Because your family deserves a bright future

Beneath this was a picture of two parents, a son, and a daughter frolicking on a hillside. The rest of the pamphlet delved into a range of subjects from HDL, LDL, triglyceride counts, and artery plaque to beneficial cooking oils and relaxation techniques. I knew all about these things. I knew my triglyceride count (145), and I knew the benefits of monounsaturated fats versus polyunsaturated, saturated, and trans. I knew the difference between isoflavones and bioflavonoids. I knew all about deep breathing. I understood these things because my parents had amassed an impressive library of health books over the years, and in the past few months I'd begun to make my way through them. The library included, but was not limited to, volumes on heart disease, assorted cancers, autoimmune conditions, intestinal disorders, the efficacy of sundry medications, preventative diets, and the meaning of vague symptoms–basically, everything that could go wrong with the human body, and a plethora of theories on how to fix it.

My sister, my father, and I used to think that my mother was a hypochondriac because she kept buying and reading these books. She always thought some strange thing might be wrong with her; throughout her life she kept going to the doctor with notebooks of her symptoms (I found them after she died–ulcers, cluster headaches, random aches and pains, indigestion, a swollen knee, canker sores). We thought she was insane. We rolled our eyes and whispered that she was crazy for worrying so much over nothing.

Over nothing.

That was what made me feel queasy now even to think about. What if we'd taken her complaints seriously? What if we'd known about melanoma–had known that it even existed? She hadn't even been in the sun that much, but we should never have let her sit on a lawn chair in our tiny yard at all.

The disease books also gave me a strange sense of companionship–we weren't the only family who'd been blindsided. It was astonishing how many diseases could be lurking in you without your knowledge, how many health hazards were waiting to sneak up on you. My father's *Health Now* newsletters were the scariest. They were filled with terrifying stories of people who'd died from eating contaminated radishes, or from a blood clot that they'd gotten from sitting too long and which had traveled to the lung. All sorts of cancers took people by surprise.

My mother hadn't been the only one to die in two weeks from what seemed at first to be nothing.

My father saved all his *Health Now* back issues, and I read them like a Stephen King novel. In addition to profiling little-known diseases, the newsletter blew the whistle on the worst cancer-causing, heart-disease-inducing foods in articles like "Ten Foods for an Early Death" and "A Sure Path to a Heart Attack." One issue had stories of *E. coli* and salmonella, and a tale called "Death from Eating a Hamburger." Another issue featured "Candy: Trick, Not a Treat," which informed me that "just one Hershey's Milk Chocolate bar looks innocent enough–but are thirty seconds of pleasure really worth half your day's saturated fat? Call it the death snack."

Death snack? I'd stared guiltily at a Twix wrapper poking out of my book bag.

July was the carcinogen issue, with its never-ending list of foes: burnt toast, shampoo, cleansers, grilled meat, peanuts, water, air. One article ended by stating: "People everywhere are unwittingly *causing their own diseases*–staying out in the sun too long, eating the wrong foods, being exposed to unfortunate chemicals."

Right after my mother died, my father took us to a dermatologist to have our skin checked, just to be sure the bad genes we'd inherited weren't already wreaking havoc, that it wasn't already too late. I lay on the dermatologist's table as he removed an atypical nevus (aka a weird-looking mole) from the skin over my stomach. I could feel the blood dripping painlessly (he'd shot it with anesthetic) and felt almost comically lackadaisical: *Eh, who cares. Whatever. If I die, I die. So what.* Dying didn't look all *that* bad.

Because, then, for a very brief period after my mother's death, when I thought of that specific nanosecond in time, it had seemed almost calm. It had seemed strangely quiet or peaceful, in retrospect–it seemed, really, like *passing*. She was there, and then she wasn't. Her body was hers, and then it was something she'd left behind.

Bashert, my mother used to say to comfort herself when someone died of natural causes, like our elementary school principal, Mrs. Kouliadades, who had breast cancer, or Mrs. Hamish across the street, of diabetes. It was Yiddish for "fate," for "meant to be"–something there was no point arguing about since there was nothing you could do, she'd said. It seemed like a word for coming to terms with things and accepting chance. Not to dwell. To move on and forget.

I said *bashert* to myself after she died, but it didn't make me feel any better. And that feeling of calmness surrounding her death hadn't lasted long–the memories of the horrible parts won out. Her suffering and vomiting, peeing the color of coffee; my sister screaming and crying; the feeling of machines grinding inside me–that's what was most vivid to me now. What were the stages described in that grief book? I couldn't remember, but I was sure that worry should be one of them.

The mole turned out to be benign, but I got scared. I started examining my moles closely and keeping detailed notes on them, as the dermatologist had instructed, on the lookout for suspicious growth or changes. I memorized the *ABCD's of Melanoma* pamphlet he'd given me.

107

Then I met the cancer guy, and my worries increased. "He was tired–that was the first sign. He had to lie down in the middle of the day. Then he had these red spots on his legs," Gigi told us in the hallway one afternoon, remembering. "It happened when he was fifteen. I called the doctor and he said to come in right away. He knew what it was off the bat, I could tell from his face. But he ordered tests before he said anything. The tests came back, and sure enough: acute lymphocytic leukemia. Next thing I know we're in the hospital."

Now, leafing through my father's Green Springs brochure, I felt tired. I checked my own legs for spots.

I was afraid that something could be in me too, ticking away, ready to strike at any moment. Or if not a disease, then an accident, coiled in the future like a cat waiting to spring. I'd lived all my life not worrying at all–never once had I worried about my mother having melanoma and dying in twelve days, or fifteen-year-olds catching fatal diseases. What an ignoramus! What a naive, unknowing, sheltered newbie.

The cancer guy had spoken to me once. It was in the solarium, the day after his birthday party. He said, "I like your dad. He's funny."

"Thanks," I said, and stared down at my book. The cancer guy was talking to me. To *me*. Why me? I tried to see myself in his eyes. It would probably make him happy to have a healthy, regular girl talk to him. I mean, what girls did he meet in here? Cancer girls?

A wave of shame engulfed me. Shame that I was thinking

these thoughts, that I kind of *liked* him, and I was afraid that the thing I liked was his cancer.

I'd watched too many TV movies–I'd always felt sorry for those young main characters–and now here was one in front of me. Dying. He was *dying.* Of *cancer.* I couldn't even wrap my mind around it. He was only four years older than me.

He was kind of cute, though, despite the baldness and pale skin.

He hovered beside me, waiting for me to say something. I forced myself to speak. "Did you, um, have a good birthday?" I asked. My voice sounded like an ad for Cheer laundry detergent.

"It was splendid," he said.

More shame, hot and sickening. I was such a doofus. To think that I found his cancer appealing, that I felt attracted to his horrifying tragedy like a gnat to light. A rubbernecker, that's what I was. I'd been so mad at Melody Bly and those who'd wanted to crash my own grief party, and now I was doing exactly the same thing.

I was disgusting. My face flushed; I gazed at my book.

"What are you reading?" he asked.

It was a romance novel entitled *Larissa's Love Royale,* which I'd bought in the gift shop. It wasn't one of those romances with a subtle cover that try to pass themselves off as ordinary books, either. No. This was all luscious bosom, gold embossed letters, and tanned male chestage, set on a Renaissance pirate ship. Why hadn't I brought *The Canterbury Tales,* which we were reading in school, instead?

Perhaps because it was hard to lose myself in *Thanne longen folk to goon on pilgrimages* in the death ward.

"Um," I said, "nothing." I kept gazing at my open book, maneuvering my arms to shield the page from his view. I was afraid to look at him. I tried to think of how to slip the novel into my book bag smoothly and non-embarrassingly when he said, "Well. Bye." And he walked back toward his room.

That was it.

I didn't even say bye back. I didn't call after him, *Wait! Sorry!* Or *Get well soon!* Or *Actually, I really like you!*

I replayed, rewrote, reimagined the scene in my head many times after that, developing it into further interactions with plot twists and revelations. In one version the cancer guy said he was in love with me and wanted one last hurrah before death. In another, he helped me with my homework while I consoled him with understanding Florence Nightingale-esque gestures and an assured knowledge of the afterlife: *I've seen death too. Don't worry. It didn't look all that bad, really.* After a while I almost believed we'd had this connection, that I'd helped him. I wanted to help him, I told myself. Secretly, though, I was nervous every time I stepped out of the elevator and walked toward my father's room, afraid to see an empty bed, to find out that the cancer guy had died. I was relieved when, the next day, my father was transferred to another room.

My father and I packed our suitcases. I used a flowered one that my mother had bought but never used; I clipped the Bloomingdale's tags off it.

"Alex is on the phone!" my father shouted just before we left. We phoned her in Ithaca every day; usually she was out.

She'd sent us a postcard that said Ithaca Is Gorges. She seemed to be having a grand old time without us.

"What's up?" she asked me.

"Nothing. I'm a little nervous."

"I know—a vacation with just you and Daddy. Sort of weird."

"Also, on long drives you're at risk for deep vein thrombosis, which could lead to pulmonary embolism and you could die. The only symptom is an achy calf—and sometimes there are no symptoms at all."

"Huh?"

"Deep—"

"You're insane. Stop reading Mommy and Daddy's disease books. I have to go," she said. "Have a good trip."

"Do you miss us?" I missed her—the house felt too empty without her sulky presence in it. We were soldiers in the combat field of our disintegrating family, and I wanted to be the one who'd deserted, not the one who'd been left behind. Sometimes I would go into her room and just look around; I'd pick up the stuffed animals she hadn't taken with her, examine the earrings left in her jewelry box. I caught my father in there once too, sitting on her bed, staring at her old sneakers.

"Yeah. Everyone's leaving for breakfast—gotta run, see you!"

We loaded up our blue Zephyr. My mother used to criticize my father's driving—he drove too fast, too close to trucks, he passed too much on the BQE—and now he seemed to drive more cautiously, out of a sudden regretful respect. He also seemed curious about me in a new way, as if I was an odd foreign being. "Who are these musicians?" he asked when I popped in my Go-Go's tape as we drove over the Verrazano Bridge. I told him their names.

"Belinda." He nodded. "She has a nice voice."

He glanced at the *Beauty and the Beat* tape case resting on the dashboard. "What the hell's all that paint on their faces?"

"It's not paint! It's a mud masque!" I shook my head. "Haven't you ever noticed me in mud masques? I've been using them since I was twelve!"

"I'm sorry," he said.

I watched New York Harbor go by in a blur. I didn't want him to like my music–it felt as if he was peeking in my journal. A few minutes later he belted out, "Everybody get on your feet, we got it!" in his gravelly, off-key voice.

I pressed the stop button.

"Don't turn it off," he said.

"No more Go-Go's. But we're not listening to any country."

I picked up Depeche Mode, but after imagining him crooning *All I ever wanted, All I ever needed,* I put on Judy Collins instead. My mother had been crazy about Judy Collins; she had all her records. I liked her voice–it was strong and sort of soothing and reminded me of my mother.

We cruised past Staten Island. My father said, "When Greta and I were courting"–Courting? I pictured a horse and carriage bouncing down a country lane, my mother in a hoop skirt–"I gave your mother a Judy Collins record. I forget which one it was. *Golden Apples*? I can't remember. Anyhow, I gave her the record, and she loved it–it wasn't an easy one to find. She was almost in tears, she was so happy to have it–she said it was the nicest gift she'd ever gotten. Later, when we moved to

Queens, I see she has two *Golden Apples*. She didn't want me to feel bad that she already had it. That's the kind of woman your mother was."

A part of me wanted to roll my eyes as usual and snap: *Thanks. That's really illuminating.* But it was. How had I not heard this story before? My mother was nice enough to lie effusively when given a double gift–that's who she was, a tiny piece to attach to the sprawling, incomprehensible puzzle of her. I envied my father for these secret nuggets of knowledge, for knowing so much more of her than I did. Sometimes I imagined that if I could stick a key into his chest it would open up like an armoire and reveal all the secrets of her life, all the stories and memories, and I could page through them and know her, really know her. My memories weren't enough. I wanted his. I once asked him, "Tell me stories about Mommy," but his face was as blank as mine when Ms. Poletti asked me to recite Sonnet 38 from memory. I had to wait for these things to come out on their own.

We drove on and I did my ankle exercises when I remembered. The city evolved into trees and towns and farmland. After we'd exhausted three Judy Collins tapes we decided to stop for lunch–we wanted to find something healthy to eat, to start our week off on a good footing. When we saw a Wendy's sign I yelled, "Pull over!" He headed into the exit lane. "They have a new grilled chicken sandwich I read about in *Health Now,*" I said.

We parked, waited on line, and ordered two grilled chickens with dry baked potatoes on the side. "No fries," I instructed.

"She's the boss," he told the cashier.

We settled into a shiny lacquered table by the window–my

father wanted to keep an eye on our car in the parking lot. He took a bite of his sandwich. "Not bad," he said.

"Kind of yummy," I said.

"Could use some butter," he mumbled over his potato.

"I should've brought the I Can't Believe It's Not Butter."

"The I *Can* Believe It's Not Butter? That stuff is *bleh,*" he said.

I'd bought it after reading a *Health Now* feature on it. "It's not *bleh*. It tastes just like butter."

"*Bleh.*"

"You need to change your attitude," I said.

A man at the table beside us eavesdropped and laughed.

I glanced around the Wendy's and wondered what these people thought of us. Who did they see, looking at us? *This isn't us, really, the two of us alone,* I wanted to tell them. *We don't know how the hell we ended up here by ourselves.*

We took our iced teas to the car, but as soon as my father started driving again I fell asleep. An hour after I woke up, we approached the Green Springs driveway.

"I guess this is it," he said.

The driveway was lined with stone walls; a guard poked his head out of a wooden booth in the middle of the road. "Healthy Heart check-ins?"

"That's us." My father told him our names, and he compared them to a list.

"Straight ahead."

The resort looked like a mansion that had hired the cast of the Golden Girls to decorate. Inside was all big pastel flowers and gilt moldings and overgrown ficuses.

We registered at the front desk and received two green folders and Hello My Name Is stickers to put on our shirts. The receptionist pointed us toward a banquet room, where an entire Golden Girls convention seemed to be taking place.

My father and I hovered by the food table, wallflowers at a school dance. I filled a plate with grapes and what looked like a hunk of cheese but tasted like an eraser.

"This is a lot of old ladies," I said, scanning the room. It was old-lady summer camp, all bouffant hair and honey-thick perfume.

"What's this, hoomis?"

"*Hummus.* It's hummus, Dad."

"Tastes like creamed sawdust."

After a while a man moved to the front and asked us to take our seats. He introduced himself as Dr. Milken.

"Welcome. We're so glad you came to Green Springs." He launched into a "health, happiness, and longevity" spiel, which suspiciously resembled the Healthy Heart brochure, and began to introduce about twenty different doctors and explain their specialties. As he droned on, my mind shifted to the cancer guy. I wanted to ask him if he ever thought about what might have caused his disease. Had he grown up near power lines? Was there something bad in their water? Pesticides?

Had he ever read *Health Now*?

I felt a sudden chill and knew for certain that I couldn't ask him. I knew the cancer guy had died. I *felt* it, the absence. He was gone—somehow I was sure of this. In my mind I watched his body being wheeled away like my mother's, Gigi picking up his hand, kissing his nose, his forehead, leaving the hospital with the plastic bag emblazoned with PATIENTS BELONGINGS in purple letters. A friend would pick her up and as she was waiting in the lobby she'd almost want to stay in this hospital where she'd spent so much time over the years, with its familiar rush of visitors, almost like a busy office building, except for all the hope and dread. And now when she walked out that door: only dread.

She'd sit in her friend's car and talk about how it was over finally–a relief. Relief? Not the right word. The friend would discuss the traffic on First Avenue, the weather, it was time for dinner, she must be hungry.

She wasn't hungry.

Had she eaten?

Not really. (An orange on Tuesday. A packet of saltines.)

She should eat. Did she feel like Chinese?

Chinese would be fine.

At the Chinese restaurant she'd think the whole time about the bag of belongings in her friend's car, that she shouldn't have left it there. She'd regret leaving it on the backseat throughout the entire dinner. What if someone broke in and took it? She'd never forgive herself if that happened.

I looked up–green folders were flipping open all around me. Dr. Milken asked us to take out a card inside that divided us into groups called "families."

"Are you okay?" my father asked. "You look lost."

I tried to find my voice. "I'm fine."

"We're in Family Three," he said, and he led me toward the designated room.

There were seven members of Family Three plus two doctors, Dr. Marcy Fishbaum, a redheaded psychologist with a bowl cut, and Dr. Henry Jackson, a cardiologist in a blue sweater with a metallic sheen that had a certain Liberace-ness about it. *You'd think with their kind of money he could buy a nice-looking sweater.*

Dr. Fishbaum asked us to go around the circle, introduce ourselves, and say what brought us to Green Springs. She asked Nikki Glimcher to start.

Nikki and her husband, Tommy, resembled two giant human dumplings. "We're in our sixties now, and I kinda had to drag Tommy here—he didn't wanna come," she said. Tommy examined the ceiling. "Six months ago, he had a heart attack." Her voice cracked; she took a deep breath.

"But no way am I gonna eat rabbit food," Tommy said.

Next was Cindy Curry from Florida; she'd come with her mother, Alva. "My husband died four years ago during a routine angioplasty," Cindy said, her friendly, seahorsey face bobbing. "And my dad died of stomach cancer five years before that."

"We have high cholesterol—runs in the family. We're on Questran," Alva said.

My father took Questran also, that chalky powder he stirred into his orange juice every morning.

Shelly Petra shifted in her seat and tugged at her gingham headband. She was the youngest person in the group besides me. "I came here from Chapel Hill. I'm a professor of anthropology at UNC." She pushed her purple-rimmed glasses back on her nose. She opened her mouth and paused for a long time. Dr. Fishbaum seemed unsure whether to move on to me, or wait for her to speak, but Shelly finally continued. "I came here by myself because Ron, my husband, passed away last year. He had a severe myocardial infarction and he was thirty-five." Long pause.

"Do you have high cholesterol or other risk factors yourself?" Dr. Jackson asked.

She shook her head. "No. But I eat a nearly fat-free diet. I'm very careful. I saw an ad for this retreat in *Health Now,* and I decided to take the plunge."

"We're glad you're here," Dr. Fishbaum said, and nodded at me.

"Um, I read *Health Now* too," I said. "I'm here with my dad. My triglyceride count is borderline high–one forty-five. I have a genetic predisposition for heart disease. And melanoma. I mean a predisposition for melanoma–I don't have it of course, ha ha ha. My mom did–she died. But my father and I are eating well. We're doing really good." I sounded awful; I should've rehearsed what I'd say while the others were speaking.

Alva clucked her tongue, and Shelly and Cindy nodded sympathetically. I couldn't believe all these people had lost someone as well. What a sorry lot we were. But people died every day, didn't they? Every minute. While we'd been sitting here hundreds of people had died. Hundreds of families were getting their hearts torn out. I couldn't fathom it. I wasn't sure how it was possible, really, all these people all over the world quietly grieving. You'd think that if everyone was going through this, you'd see them all on the street in a communal howl. There'd be grief riots, Healthy Grief Week, and grief spas. Grief mud masques. Grief nail polish.

My father was saying, "I've had two heart attacks in my life now, and triple bypass. Well, as my daughter said, my wife died in January. My health is good! I'm in good shape. My daughter's watching my diet. We had a Wendy's grilled chicken on the way down–no fries–and the chicken wasn't half bad."

"I'm glad you brought up the subject of healthy eating," Dr. Fishbaum said. "We're going to start with a simple exercise tonight, to begin the process of examining our lifestyles closely, to make room for change."

We were supposed to recall everything we'd eaten in the last three days, to the best of our memory. I felt virtuous, writing it. No Twixes, fries, or burgers for me of late. Even at the Queens Burger I'd been eating simple pastas and the vegetable plate after my shift.

Nikki Glimcher whispered to her husband, "Don't lie! You had three Big Macs!"

"What's in the past is in the past. We're making room for change in the future," Dr. Fishbaum said.

"Thing is, I'll eat the rabbit food and make myself miserable and then I'll probably get sideswiped the next day by an eighteen-wheeler on I-78 like my uncle Jarvis," Tommy said. Nikki glared at him.

But I thought he had a point. In the end my father's death would probably not come from a heart attack, and I wouldn't get melanoma–no, that would be too expected. It would be something else–a staph infection, an aneurysm, pneumonia. I'd read of people who'd died unexpectedly from all these things, how their families were shocked by the cruel twist.

Dr. Jackson had an answer: "Wear a seatbelt and drive cautiously."

That night, while my father was in his initial stress evaluation consultation, I unpacked my things in our room. Then I picked up the phone and dialed information.

"What city?" the operator asked.

"New York."

"What listing?"

"A residence–Gigi Backus."

"There's a Gigi Backus on Degraw Street in Brooklyn."

"I'll try that." I could picture her house with plastic-covered couches and embroidered wall hangings and a hairy white cat.

I wrote down the number. What did I want to say? That I was sorry about her son? That I was sorry I hadn't said bye to him? That I just wanted to make sure she was okay? Maybe I'd tell her that I'd liked him.

I was still deciding what to say when the answering machine clicked on.

"This is Gigi! Not here right now 'cause I'm out on the town! Please leave a message–don't just hang up! I hate it when people just hang up." *Beep.*

I hung up.

I glanced at my bare legs: no spots. It was crazy to worry so much; I knew that. But the loss of control galled me. You simply got picked to die. It seemed no different than in Shirley Jackson's "The Lottery," which we'd read in English class—a public stoning.

Worry was something to do, an occupation at least. A part of me actually felt it might help. If only I had worried before, maybe we could've prevented some things. Maybe now we'd be on the lookout for staph infections, aneurysms, eighteen-wheelers.

Maybe worry could save your life. And if it didn't—if you didn't catch the disease early enough, or avoid the oncoming truck—if you could prepare for the worst, maybe it might make it a little easier. Maybe worrying, thinking about these diseases, would make you feel more ready. You'd expect it. You wouldn't feel so sideswiped, so surprised. You'd have control—even if only a tiny, tiny bit.

We quickly fell into the routine of Green Springs: whole-grain breakfasts; the morning Family Meeting, during which we discussed the obstacles we faced in lifestyle change; exercise classes (my father swam, I did step aerobics); then afternoon and evening health lectures.

My father was a gung-ho student, taking pages of notes in all classes on everything from gingko biloba to the benefits of craniosacral massage. He used to hate that kind of stuff. When my mother's friends had called with tips from alternative-medicine books and New-Age newsletters, suggesting everything from watching sitcoms to sprinkling cornmeal in our yard to make my mother better, he'd scoffed. He'd called it their woo-woo advice. (Woo-woo said with a wave of the hand, a fruity expression.)

Now my father leaned over to me during the Alternative

Supplements Workshop and said, "Maybe Mommy should've tried the shark cartilage."

At meals we were encouraged to sit with our Families, though my father and I quickly discovered we preferred to eat by ourselves, without the others' incessant complaining. They all kvetched about the lack of butter and alcohol, the strange foods and fibrousness. Discussions frequently centered on everyone's "daily eliminations"— as in "Due to increased fiber intake, your eliminations may be substantially larger than you're used to," which was what Dr. Milken announced in a lecture our second day. "My elimination was *way, way* larger than I'm used to!" Tommy said at dinner that night.

My father and I preferred not to discuss the quality and quantity of our eliminations. Plus, I liked the food. I was in *Health Now* menu heaven. I liked the tofu, tempeh, seitan, texturized vegetable protein, and ground flaxseeds, and best of all, every meal was included in the price, so I could have whatever I wanted off the menu without guilt. The spa made money off this, my father maintained, since most everyone there was dieting. But not me. Blessed with a good metabolism, I ordered two appetizers, two entrees, and two desserts at each meal, plus I made endless salad bar voyages. My father grinned. "Thank God we're getting our money's worth."

I was on my second dessert–a chocolate chip oatmeal flax cookie–on our third night when my father said, "Uh-oh. Golden Girls alert." Alva and Cindy were walking toward our table, clucking their tongues.

"I just love watching you eat! Where does it go? Oh, I used

to eat like that when I was fifteen, just like you, and not gain a pound," Cindy said.

Alva shook her head. "At fifteen you were bigger than a sixty-nine Caddy."

Cindy ignored her. "Just don't get too used to that appetite or you'll have a hineybumper the size of Alaska in ten years!"

"You bet your bippy I won't," I said. I'd collected these words, *hineybumper* and *bippy*, from Alva and Cindy, and I was determined to use them whenever I could.

Cindy laughed and they left the dining room. I glanced around the tables. I'd begun to actually like being around all the old people. There was something comforting about their makeup and pastel leggings, flower-printed tote bags and big hair. They gave me an odd sort of hope. You could live a long time, you could endure; not everyone had to die young.

I woke up early on our fourth morning and took a bath. In the tub, I noticed a mole at the edge of my armpit had turned black. It was bigger, too. Was I imagining it? My blood pounded. I got out of the bath, put on a towel, and studied the mole in the mirror. I was definitely *not* imagining it. It looked reddish black and bulbous and different from every other mole. I hadn't brought my mole notes, but I was certain it had changed. My stomach sank as I fished out the measuring tape from the complimentary sewing kit and measured it–seven millimeters.

Holy fucking shit.

Asymmetry, borders, color, diameter—those were the melanoma ABCD's. This was asymmetrical, its color was freakish, and it was fucking *huge*.

Shit. *Shit.*

My father was already at breakfast; I sat down and showed it to him. "Don't worry yet," he said. "Let's talk to Dr. Fishbaum." My father didn't seem too nervous—just quietly concerned. He was probably used to disease now, after his two heart attacks and our mother. It was old hat.

"I've been really tired lately too," I said, breathing deeply. "Fatigued."

"Eat some breakfast."

"I'm not hungry."

"Try some oatmeal." He pushed his bowl toward me, and I took a few bites. It tasted like soggy cardboard. Then I convinced him to leave breakfast early and look for Dr. Fishbaum.

We found her in her office, drinking a cup of coffee and reading the newspaper.

"Excuse me," my father said. "We're sorry to interrupt. My daughter found a strange mole, and we'd like to see a dermatologist, if that's possible." He sounded so calm; I was almost in tears.

She gave me an empathetic glance. She knew the details of my mother's melanoma and quick death from our Family Meetings, and she'd proved to be a much more understanding member of the counseling field than Gina Petrollo. "I'll see what I can do," she said.

I tried not to think about it. *It's nothing*, I told myself. Then: *This is it. It's over.* Would it be twelve days, like my mother? Or years, like the cancer guy? I'd known this would happen. That's what life was—you'd be going along fine, and poof! It was all gone. There was absolutely nothing that could ensure that you'd be okay, that you'd be lucky. That's what it all boiled down to: luck, or lack thereof.

I'm not ready to die, I thought. *I can't do it.* But who was I to expect to be spared? I wasn't safe or protected, and that tiny, tiny bit of control didn't exist—it was just another scrap of delusion. I spaced out during Family Meeting, at the Cooking with Seitan demonstration my hands were shaking, and in aerobics class I kept stopping and messing up all the moves. I'd grow hot, sweaty, and shivery, start to panic about dying, then convince myself I'd be okay. Then I'd panic again.

At lunchtime Dr. Fishbaum came over to our table and said I had an appointment with Dr. Morris at 3 p.m. at the Green Springs Health Annex, and later that afternoon my father drove me to Dr. Morris's office. "You should get back," I said. "You're missing the soybean lecture."

"No, I'll wait."

I hugged him. I braced myself as the nurse led me into the examining room and I put on the huge blue paper gown. A few minutes later Dr. Morris appeared and introduced himself. "Nice to meet you, Miss Pearlman."

I nodded and tried to breathe.

He read the questionnaire I'd filled out. "You have a growth that's causing you concern?"

I nodded again, and showed him the mole under my arm. "What is it?" I rasped.

Dr. Morris took one glance at it and smiled. "It's benign."

I squinted at him. "Are you sure?"

He inspected it again. "Have you had it for a long time?"

"Yeah, but it's changed. It never looked like that before."

"Did you shave under your arms recently?"

"I–I guess so. Maybe."

"You most likely nicked the mole with the razor and didn't realize it. Don't worry–I'm positive it's benign." He put a cream on it and placed a Band-Aid over the spot.

I felt limp and almost relieved, but I didn't entirely believe him. "What about my fatigue?"

"Have you been sleeping well?"

It had been hard to fall asleep at night with my father snoring. "It's just–I worry that I have it undetected, like my mother. One of her doctors said it could've been growing undetected for twenty years. And I've read about people getting melanoma really young. A girl who was sixteen died from it–and a guy who was nineteen."

"It happens," he said.

"It happens"? Is that it?

"You're fair-skinned and have a high number of atypical nevi, but just because your mother died of melanoma doesn't mean you will."

"What can I do to prevent it? Beyond staying out of the sun?"

He shrugged. "Eat broccoli?" His frown unfurled like an umbrella. "There are some things beyond our control, unfortunately. You're doing a good job keeping away from the sun," he said, surveying my so-pale-it-was-almost-see-through skin. "The link between melanoma and sunlight isn't even definitively proven, but it's a good idea to keep doing what you're doing, to prevent squamous and basal cell carcinomas as well."

Great. More cancers to worry about. He closed my folder, and I thanked him and returned to the waiting room. "It's fine," I told my father. "I–um–I cut it shaving, I guess."

He grinned and hugged me, then paid the bill without even a peep about the expense. Dr. Morris popped back out to hand me a catalog of sun-protective clothing. The clothes resembled astronaut suits.

My father said, "Do they make that in a miniskirt?"

I was thankful that everything was all right, but as we drove back to the spa I cringed, feeling humiliated. I'd become a hypochondriac. A big ball of fear and worry and stupidness. I used to read my sister's *National Geographic* magazines and dream of doing exciting things like climbing mountains and traveling to Madagascar and Australia and petting koalas–and now my dream was just not to die young. What kind of a dream was that? How would that look on my college applications? An essay about hoping not to kick the bucket from cancer or meningitis or flesh-eating bacteria, about the benefits of omega-3's and polyphenols?

Back in our room, alone, before dinner, I tried Gigi's number once more.

"Hello?"

I wasn't expecting her to pick up. "Um, hi . . . this is . . . I'm not sure if you remember me . . . this is Mia Pearlman. My dad–Simon Pearlman–"

"Oh! Of course I remember you! How are you? Oh, no. Oh, God. Did your–your dad–?"

"No–no, he's great, he's totally fine. I'm just calling because–I was thinking of Sasha and–" I paused. How could I say it? I hated the phrase *I'm sorry. So sorry about your son.* It was such a stupid expression. Why had no one ever come up with a better one? Such as: *What a fucking load of crap you've been dealt. Really.* Then I remembered.

"Bashert," I said. "About Sasha."

"Huh?"

"It's this Yiddish word for fate. My mom used to say it."

"I know! How did you hear? Did Dr. Kornovoy tell you? Did you run into him? I couldn't believe it myself. It's crazy. I know. Your father must think I'm off my rocker for letting him go. But Dr. Kornovoy gave his permission. I even paid for the Eurail pass. I know, I'm crazy to do it. I tried to convince him not to. But you only get one life, right? That's what they say, right? I'm making an album from his postcards, and I'm going to add the pictures when he gets back. Paris, Venice, I got so far. Amsterdam. He's in Amsterdam right now. I wish I was there with him, but he's nineteen, he can't have his mom by his side all the time, you know, right? Anyway, so you ran into Dr. Kornovoy at NYU?"

"I–" I didn't know what to say. I paused, speechless. "Yeah."

"I'm so happy you called. I wondered how your dad was doing. Not that long ago I said to Sasha, 'Remember that nice Simon and his daughters?' Sasha liked your dad so much. You spend time in that hospital, so intense, right? And then just disappear and not know what's doing. Anyway, give me your number, we'll keep in touch. Please give my love to your dad. It was so nice of you to call."

"I will." I gave her our number and address.

Three days later, when my father and I were back home, I looked up *bashert* in one of my parents' Yiddish dictionaries. It meant "predestined" and "fate," but it had another meaning as well: "the person with whom you were meant to be." A soul mate, as in "I have found my *bashert*," the dictionary said. And it seemed right that the same word could be used in instances of both love and death.

How to
Find Love

She is a friend of my mind. . . . The pieces I am, she gather them and give them back to me in all the right order.

—Toni Morrison
Beloved

HOW DO YOU fall in love?

This was what I awoke wondering the morning I turned sixteen. It was early September, during one of New York's record heat waves; even my bedroom windows seemed to sweat. When I opened my eyes all I could think was that it wouldn't be so bad to wake up sweating if you awoke beside somebody else.

But there wasn't anyone else. In our quiet, empty house, my single bed was filled only with pancake-flat, fur-mangled stuffed animals. Lately my father had been trying to get me to throw them out; he'd finally given up the night before, when I stood before my bears, rabbits, gorillas, and kangaroos and, with all the passion of Scarlett O'Hara, vowed in a fierce, husky voice, *"Never."*

But now all I could think was that I was a sixteen-year-old girl still sleeping with gorillas. Not like *Sixteen Candles*, or any of those kinds of movies; there were no boyfriends or hopes of boyfriends waiting outside my door. I felt my skin grow hot as I thought of my recent crushes: Jay Kasper, Richard Bridgewald, and the healthy person formerly known as the

135

cancer guy. Sometimes I wanted to edit my life, run it all on a film monitor and instruct, "Cut this, cut that," and it would all piece together so much more smoothly.

Sweet sixteen.

Birthdays had been a big deal when I was little: parties with tons of kids pinning the tail on the donkey, batting piñatas, gorging on Betty Crocker SuperMoist cake with fudge frosting. My mother always bought the gifts—a three-tiered set of Ultima II makeup last year, silver-plated hair clips the year before.

This year I knew what my father had gotten me, because he'd left it in a bag in the hall closet—Teen Lady shampoo, body wash, and scented powder from the supermarket. He must've asked the store clerk what to get for a *girl*, and been told this. I'd begun to wish there was some guidebook I could give him, *How to Raise a Daughter* or something; he still seemed near cardiac arrest when I asked for money for tampons, had yet to show a glimmer of comprehension of the magic word *shopping*, and thought reupholstering the couch made for a fun Saturday night. In fact, the couch was now his whole existence; he'd decided to retire on my mother's life insurance money, and put the shop up for sale. He now spent each day on the couch reading the complete *New York Times*. He was like a clipping service without the paying clients.

Every afternoon when I came home from school he'd narrate his day: "This morning I had myself a bagel with the no-fat cream cheese, lunch a Wendy's grilled chicken. In Topeka they had a scandal with the honey mustard sauce, people got sick—I read it on page six of the Living section, I saved the article for you," and I'd gaze longingly at the television, as if I could jump into a family on the set. At Green Springs he'd bought a *Yoga for Relaxation* videotape, and before bed each night he'd lie on the living room rug, palms upward, as New Age music floated through the room.

Aside from the Wendy's cashiers, I was often the only person he talked to during the day. "Why don't you bring your friends over? I'll bake a chicken," he'd ask me on the weekends. Or "Invite Sarah, we'll play Scrabble," "Mimi can help us fix the bird feeder," or "I bet Rebecca would like this Sherlock Holmes movie too." It didn't matter that I hadn't seen Sarah, Mimi, or Rebecca since fifth grade, or that if I asked them over now, they'd surely run off–our house had become Spooky House, one of those run-down, weedy, crumbling places that's the nightmare of every kid on the block. We never uprooted dead plants or picked up the litter from the yard, and inside, funeral casseroles still filled the freezer, my mother's clothes hung in the closets, and bags of supplies from her office sat unpacked in the basement. We hadn't even thrown out her magazines or her used-up shampoos, as if we feared even the dust would shift.

I'd also made a scrapbook of her, pasting in photos, birthday cards, letters, the obituary. I'd started a ritual of leafing through it before I went to bed at night.

It was still an hour before I had to leave for school, but I got dressed and left the house. I lingered at the newsstand by the subway, and there I saw it, gleaming at me from the cover of *Cosmopolitan*: "How to Find Love." I devoured it during my subway ride to school.

HOW to FIND LOVE

Love may *happen* to some women—goddesses, movie stars, models—knights descend on them, scooping them onto white horses, hunks of the month call and ask them for dates. But the rest of us have to go out and *find* our true loves.

It isn't as hard as you think. He's out there; you just have to look for him. If you seem friendly and receptive, someone will notice and take an interest in you. So here's the secret to finding love: get out there, make yourself available, be *open* to love! Here are some places to start your search.

Libraries. Find an attractive man and ask, "How do I use this microfiche?"

Grocery stores. Check his shopping cart and ask where he got the fresh basil. (Stay away from men with tampons in their carts—they're spoken for.)

Hospitals. A wealth of opportunities here: doctors, medical students, patients—they do recover!

Car shows. Men flock to them . . .

"What the hell kind of guy are you gonna meet at a car show, someone from *Grease*? Danny Zucco? Kenickie?" a voice said over my shoulder. It was Kelsey Kang, my Spanish Level Two deskmate. I hadn't noticed when she'd gotten on the train, I'd been so engrossed in the article, and it was strange seeing her on the subway; I'd never seen her outside of school before. Mornings on the 7 train were always the worst, most crowded time, and in the hot weather it only grew smellier.

I smiled at her and stuffed the magazine into my book bag, embarrassed to have been caught reading it. What if she thought I was desperate?

But I was desperate. I was always daydreaming, getting a crush on some guy. Unrequited or not, during even the most awful day a crush could change everything–it could make you forget the two classes you failed last semester, and the general overall suckiness of your life. A crush removed the world, at least for a little while.

And it wasn't so different with friendships. At Grand Central several passengers got up and we took their seats, and I loved the thought of riding the subway with Kelsey, walking the long blocks to school beside her. I stared at our reflections in the darkened window. I wanted a best friend as much as a boyfriend, someone I could talk to about everything. But was it a myth, that kind of friend? A myth like having a mother was a myth, or a father like the ones on TV?

Kelsey glanced at her watch. "How come you're going to school so early?"

I shrugged. "I woke up early." I didn't want to say that it was my birthday, that I had nothing special going on. "What about you?"

"I usually get to school early to do homework. I never have time after school–I work at my parents' store or am making dinner for my stupid brothers or something. I'm a nerd now," she added with a resigned sigh, though with her sleek black hair and high-heeled boots she clearly wasn't. "I'm turning over a new leaf. You really just woke up early?" She looked at me oddly, as if she couldn't imagine a stranger thing to do.

"Well, actually . . . " Why not just say it? "It's my birthday."

Her eyes lit up. "Happy birthday! How old are you?"

"Sixteen."

"What do you have planned? Are you having a sweet sixteen?"

"I don't think so." My father and I hadn't made any plans except for eating the Sara Lee cake in the freezer. "It's not such a big deal."

"It is," Kelsey said. "The last place you should be on your birthday is in school."

I nodded. Aside from the unbearably dull classes and diabolical teachers, the building itself was miserable–the soiled bathrooms, the cafeteria that smelled like cold oatmeal and cottage cheese. Then there were the guards who wouldn't let you in without your ID card, and the whole prisonlike, nameless, faceless state of being in high school.

At the Fifth Avenue station, we walked down the corridor to switch to the D train. "I know what we should do today," Kelsey said. "We should hang out in a supermarket and ask some guy where he got the basil."

"Or we could stroll around a hospital, looking for cute patients," I said. I didn't admit that I'd already done that, sort of.

"I always wanted to be a candy striper."

"We should do it. We should stay out until we fall in love."
I said it jokingly, but Kelsey looked up.

"It's Friday," she said. "Not much happening–no tests or anything. Nothing due. Did you have breakfast yet? I *am* kind of hungry. . . . "

I imagined it, the two of us off on our own, roaming around the city. "Have you been to Manhattan Bakery?" I said. "It's right near here. They have the best croissants in the world."

Before we could change our minds we were out on the street.

Businessmen marched up Fifth like a gray tweed parade; we strode to the bakery and gazed at the pastries rising like a hundred half-moons in the window. We bought three croissants–chocolate, almond, and regular–and shared them in the park, digging our fingers into the soft, buttery insides, pulling out puffs of cotton. How good they tasted, how good everything tastes when you're not supposed to be eating it, when right then we should've been saying *hola* to Mrs. Torres.

We walked up to Central Park and bought a romance novel at the Strand carts; at the Sheep Meadow we lay reading in the grass, skipping to the good parts, watching Frisbees slice up the sun. Kelsey read aloud:

> Tristan reached his hand down to Anastasia's furry domain. He let it rest there, as the sensations swelled and swarmed through her tawny thighs and womanly petals . . .

I groaned.

She smiled. "My sister and I own more at home. Three shelves."

"I have two shelves of them."

We saw a movie at the Paris Theatre, with subtitles and a plot neither of us understood, and we took the train to the Village, where we could shop.

Shopping: a girl's true cure for any ailment of the soul. It had begun to rain lightly, and we wandered through the dampened Village streets, pausing in stores, admiring clothes in shop windows, buying earrings from the umbrella-covered street vendors, sharing honey-roasted peanuts beneath an awning, the sweetness whirling out from the cart like a cloud.

We bought sleek black barrettes, the same kind, and silver rings with imitation rubies; we huddled under an umbrella and laughed at the crazy people walking by, muttering; we dipped our fingers into the peanut bag and clutched our packages by our sides.

I was enamored of her elegant stance and her effortless beauty, which she didn't even seem aware of; her easy laughter, trying on a leopard-print prom dress and velvet pillbox hat; the way her eyes darkened and widened as she spoke; and the circles underneath her eyes, like a sadness.

We shared bits of ourselves in passing:

My father sold gum on the streets of Seoul to put himself through college, and what was the fucking point of it, to own a goddamn store?

I wish my father'd reopen his shoe repair shop and get off

the damn couch. I almost even miss the stories of everyone's
smelly feet and bunions and corns. . . .

This old Jewish man steals from us. Bread stuffed in his
shirt. My mother lets him because she feels sorry for him. . . .

Oh my God, what if he's my father?

Clutching our packages, we stopped in Roy Rogers for dinner. We loaded our sandwiches up high and took them to the top section, which we had all to ourselves. "We still haven't met our true loves," she said.

I glanced at my watch. "I think the libraries are closed." It was already five o'clock; my father was probably home on the couch, ready to tell me how his grilled chicken was.

"Do you have to be home at a certain time?"

"No," I said, thinking of the cake holding vigil in the freezer. We hadn't set a specific hour for when we'd eat it; it was surely still frozen rock-hard in its foil pan. "Maybe I should call my father," I said.

I fished out a quarter and used the pay phone by the entrance. "Daddy? It's me. I'm out with my friend Kelsey. I think I'm going to be home a little late, okay?"

I hadn't been out late since Jay Kasper. I half expected him, like my mother had, to launch into a barrage of questions–wanting the full itinerary, with phone numbers, addresses, exact latitude and longitude of where I'd be–but he didn't. He told me happy birthday, and then said, "You're going to miss *Murder, She Wrote*."

"Oh. Well."

"I can tape it for you. Do you want me to tape *The Cosby Show* too?"

"Sure . . . thanks."

He yawned and told me to have a good time, and we hung up.

Back at the table I asked Kelsey, "What about you? Do you have to call your parents?"

She shook her head. "They keep the store open till midnight; usually they don't get home till one. I never even see them. I could stay out all night and they wouldn't notice–it's fine as long as I don't wake them up, barging in at two." She smiled. "Let's do that–let's stay out all night."

I nodded. "Until our womanly petals bloom."

We didn't have to enter a hospital, a supermarket, or a car show; we only had to sit in the Tenth Street Bar for fifteen minutes before two men approached us. Miraculous, I thought.

"You must be a wonderful Spanish teacher," Gil was saying to Kelsey. Gil and Corky: Corky was mine. They sounded like the names of goldfish, but they were handsome, they were gorgeous, they were *men*. They were from London, recent university grads, on vacation in New York for three nights.

Kelsey laughed delightedly. She'd clearly done this before; she'd said we'd have no problem sneaking in, they never carded, and she was right. The two men were swallowing her stories as eagerly as their drinks: she was a Spanish teacher at a high school, she'd told them, and, staring into her Black Bunny beer, explained that I was studying to be a vet.

I'd sipped half my gin and tonic, but already I could feel it. "Ready for another?" Corky asked.

I shook my head. "Work tomorrow," I said gravely.

"Veterinary medicine–I imagine that must be a rewarding profession."

"Oh, it is. You get that sick bunny on the examining table and–oh, it's rewarding."

What the hell were we doing? It was thrilling and exciting (were these men really taking us seriously? Could they really be interested in *us*?), but it also made me feel a little ill and frightened, as if we were crossing over into territory I wanted to enter, but wasn't sure how. Earlier, in Central Park, Kelsey and I'd mutually confessed our virginities, and agreed we'd wait until we fell in love. This wasn't love with these men, that much was clear, but it was intimidating just the same. It was one thing to read romance novels and another to have the physical fact of a man right there, itching to get into your furry domain.

"Have you been in class all day?" Gil asked.

"No," Kelsey said. "We've been celebrating Mia's twenty-second birthday. *Feliz cumpleaños!*"

She and Gil raised their glasses, and Corky bought me another drink. The clock ticked away, midnight, one. Kelsey told them about relaxing in Sheep Meadow, and the movie, and shopping, as if she and I'd been friends for years.

"Do you do this on your birthday every year? Make it a full holiday?" Corky asked me.

"Kind of," I said, and for the first time I thought of my previous birthday, before my mother got sick. She'd bought me half a cake from a gourmet shop in Manhattan, because she didn't have time to make one, and she figured we never ate the whole thing anyway. She'd placed it on the table and I'd peered around it, looking for the other half. "What happened? Did you get hungry?" I'd asked her, and she shook her head and blushed, saying it was expensive and she'd thought half seemed like a better idea. I'd sulked, feeling sorry for my measly half-cake, and I could kill myself now for not appreciating it then. Why had it seemed so imperfect?

And why, in the morning when I'd awoken, had my memories of past birthdays been so sugarcoated? Why had I not thought of the less-than-perfect ones too? I hated the way these types of memories still haunted me, dredging themselves up, unwarranted, constantly poking through–*remember me, remember me*–when I didn't want to remember any of them.

I stared at the floor. Tears brimmed in my eyes, and I blinked them back, but they poured out anyway; I cried into my drink. This *always* happened–it was pathetic. I was a professional weeper; if they had a course in it at school, I'd excel in something besides hygiene for once. I cried on every holiday, on Mother's Day, her birthday, and the seventeenth of every month, the anniversary of her death.

Corky looked horrified; he stood back. "What's wrong?"

I shook my head.

"What's up with her?" Gil asked Kelsey, as if I was some kind of freak. Kelsey didn't answer; she put her hand on my shoulder and waited for me to stop crying, which I didn't. We went to the bathroom for a tissue, and when we came out the two men had left.

We sat on the wooden bench in the subway station, waiting for the train to take us home. "Why did you do that?" Kelsey asked. "Why did you start crying?"

I shrugged. We hadn't spoken since we'd left the bar. I looked around the station. It was surprisingly packed, but only with men. A big toothless guy paced by us back and forth, leering like he was hungry and we were lunch. *Perhaps we're just going to die,* I thought, and at two in the morning this began to sound good: then the humiliation would end.

I stared at the tracks. "I don't know."

After a few moments she said, "Where's your mom? You've never talked about her."

My heart jumped, as it did whenever anybody asked; each time it was still a surprise. I shrugged. I looked down at the floor. Scuff on my black shoes. Snickers wrapper. Discarded gum. *She's in the cemetery, decomposing,* I once thought to say. But I said the usual: "She died in January," as if giving the month made it real. It didn't. Eight months had passed and here I was, the words still crumbled into me, hollow breaking lumps, screws in the chest, never-ending.

"I'm sorry."

She didn't say anything else, just looked at me, but not in an odd, surprised way–she looked at me plainly, like she was taking me in. Like she was waiting for me to say something more. And that plainness surprised me. I stared back at my shoes, the dirty ground. What was the purpose of it, all the crying, the heartbreak? I'd ruined our chances with those guys, I'd ruined our perfect day, I'd ruined *love*.

"I'm sorry I made those guys run off." I sniffed.

"They were creeps–I'm glad you did."

I wiped my nose on my sleeve; a few latent sobs were still working their way out.

"I've cried in the worst places, too," she said quietly as the train finally pulled into the station. "When my parents first opened the store, I cried nearly every day, I couldn't understand why they were working such long hours. I thought each morning when they left that they were never coming back."

"But you were like six or seven."

She shrugged. "It doesn't matter."

At Queensborough Plaza, three stops before my house and six before hers, Kelsey checked her watch. "It's almost three. My parents'll kill me if I come home now and wake them up. Do you mind–can I stay at your house?"

"Oh, sure," I croaked, horror rising in my throat at the idea. How could I bring her to Spooky House? But I didn't have a choice; I couldn't say no. I braced myself during the rest of the ride and cringed as we walked the three long blocks from the subway to my house, past the weeds, the litter, the slanting trees, the overgrown roots cracking the sidewalk, the peeling paint on our red stoop. That stoop I'd played on, hiked up jauntily so many years, and now winced to even look at.

I drew in my breath as we entered our dark living room. Pillows and newspapers were strewn on the floor; dirty mugs, plates, and the partly eaten Sara Lee cake cluttered the coffee table. My father was asleep on the couch in his sweatpants and undershirt; he woke up when I shut the door, and blinked at us. For a moment he seemed alarmed, and then confused, and then he just looked awkward, and I wondered if he was thinking, *Oh,* now *she brings a friend over, at last, at three in the morning.*

He pulled his button-down shirt off the chair and buttoned it off-kilter, so it hung about him loosely, like a smock. He hadn't shaved in days. There was dried ketchup on the pocket of his shirt. The hair he usually brushed over his bald spot hung down one side of his face, like a new-wave haircut. I told him we were at a party that ended late, and introduced them to each other.

"You'd like some coffee, Leslie?" my father said.

"Kelsey," I said.

"Kell-see. Kell-see. A slice of cake? Skim milk?"

I shook my head. "Maybe in the morning. I'm sorry. We're really tired."

But Kelsey was eyeing the chocolate cake. "I'd love a slice," she said.

So the three of us sat there, on our living room couch, drinking skim milk and eating birthday cake (it was still partly frozen in the middle) off yellow napkins imprinted with WENDY'S. My father pulled my birthday presents out of a grocery bag beneath the table; they were wrapped in newspaper and tied with a bow of string.

"Oh wow," I said, tearing off the paper, "Teen Lady. I love them." My father seemed pleased; we said good night, and I led Kelsey upstairs to my room, all the time waiting for her to revolt, to refuse to be with me any longer in my crazy, decrepit house.

I opened the door to my room—the old single bed, the satiny star mobile, the Rob Lowe poster, the Barbies. I hated it, our frozen house, my stupid childhood room, which I'd never changed or redecorated; I was never able to part with a damn thing. I thought we'd go to bed quickly: I gave her a tooth-brush, nightgown, and towel and set up the chair bed, but she didn't seem ready to sleep.

The scrapbook, the one of my mother, lay on the shelf beside my bed; she picked it up. My heart flinched to watch her open the quilted cover: there were my insides, spilling out on the page. I was embarrassed for her to see this raw, doting, unharnessed outpouring. My mother, in every period of her life, and every year of mine. Ridiculous things, I'd pasted in there: not just the birthday cards and postcards, which might be all right, but I'd included a doodle on a Post-it, a price tag from a skirt we'd bought together, a grocery list in her hand-writing, a wrapper from her favorite Fannie Farmer chocolate bar. Even December's phone bill was in there. My father had given it to me so I could check my calling-card charges, to ensure that AT&T hadn't ripped us off. Three minutes, a call to her office had been. Two minutes. One. I couldn't remem-ber where I'd called from or what we'd talked about, only that I should've talked longer.

Kelsey fingered the plastic sheets, touching it all.

"You're lucky," she said. "You're lucky to have had her."

I sat beside her. It was the first time anyone had ever said that to me.

She lay back in bed, and we stared up at the shapes in the peeled-off paint of the ceiling. We lay in the quiet, and I thought that this was what she meant by lucky: simply this.

Seduce Me

nything worth doing well is worth doing slowly.

—Gypsy Rose Lee

I NEARLY HAD a heart attack when I found the box of condoms in my father's toilet kit.

I looked away, then back again. I hoped I'd imagined it, but there they were, staring up at me: Trojans, lubricated, ribbed, extra thin for extra pleasure. Oh, God, I didn't want to think about it.

It was November, and I was on my way to visit him in the hospital again. It had become our home away from home. "My vacation spot," my father called it. "Better than Green Springs." His latest complication was an arrhythmia; the doctors had implanted a pacemaker-defibrillator, which stuck out from his waist like a deck of cards. He'd been in and out of the hospital over the last month as they made adjustments; this time he'd forgotten his toilet kit at home. Before I left the house I called Kelsey and told her about the discovery.

"Maybe he needs them to, you know, do it on his own," she said. "It's probably more sanitary that way."

"You think my father's *masturbating*?"

"Shh. Your whole neighborhood doesn't have to know. And every guy does it." She spoke with the authority of having caught her two brothers at it many a time. "Or maybe he's not, though," she considered. "Maybe he's got somebody."

"Like who? A girlfriend? Who would go out with my father?"

"What do you think he does when we go to parties on Saturday nights, or when you sleep at my house?"

"He stays at home and watches *Murder, She Wrote*. I think." My voice wavered; maybe she was right, maybe he did have some woman on the sly. I never really thought of what he did when I wasn't there; I just assumed it was the same thing he did when I was there, which was to mope around the house and read the newspaper. For the past two days, while he was in the hospital, I'd slept at Kelsey's house at night and savored my solitude in the afternoons: sprawled on our living room couch, I ate chocolate chip cookies for lunch, watched steamy soap operas, applied Deep Sea mud masque, and painted my toenails as I talked endlessly on the phone.

I said good-bye to Kelsey and left for New York University Medical Center.

The first thing I saw in his room was an empty pizza box from Earthly Delites lying on his bed tray. I'd brought sliced melon and turkey sandwiches from the corner deli; I set the grocery bag down. "You got pizza delivered?" I asked, not knowing you could do that in a hospital.

"It's cheeseless. Sylvia brought it," he said. He nodded at a woman with thick, elbow-length dyed blond hair sitting on a plastic green chair in the corner.

She glanced up from her *Astrological Times*. She was

wearing sunglasses; she took them off to glimpse me, then put them back on. "It's so sunny," she said. "Not easy on the glaucoma." My father introduced us.

"How do you two know each other?" I asked.

His face lit up with pure wonder. "We met three weeks ago, after they put the pacemaker in. They'd just released me, and I got off the elevator on the seventeenth floor by mistake– I didn't realize it was going up instead of down. I stepped out, and there she was." He grinned.

"Sylvia has lung cancer," he continued matter-of-factly. "She never smoked. It's in remission now–she's very healthy." Despite that statement he went on to catalog her additional ailments: allergies to wool, rice, strawberries, peanuts, and eggs, and white sugar didn't settle well with her either. "Sylvia and I have a lot in common," he concluded. "Anyway, she knew her surgery would go well because she asked her garoo first."

"Her what?" I asked. Her kangaroo?

"It wasn't the guru," Sylvia said. "It was the tarot cards." She turned to me. "He gets it all mixed up. I only called the Psychic Network once. I read tarot cards myself."

My father's eyes widened with excitement. "But the garoo was right–he said to go in for the surgery three weeks ago, and she did. The day after, she met me." He beamed.

"You met three weeks ago?" I couldn't believe my father had met another woman, and all this time I hadn't known.

"We did!" Sylvia said. "The Magician card came up–it means a great love or marriage is impending. I didn't under-stand it then," she went on, her eyes sparkling, "but I do now."

159

My stomach turned over. I excused myself and went into the hallway to call Kelsey.

"My father's sleeping with a clairvoyant," I said on the pay phone.

"You still can't be sure if he's sleeping with anybody. Maybe he just got the condoms as wishful thinking. Like most guys."

I felt something queer rise in my throat. "Let's just not talk about it anymore."

Our conversation moved on to Cover Girl Nail Slicks and new shoes, but I couldn't stop thinking of Sylvia. I'd known that my father would start dating sometime. It was even natural. Perhaps I'd even hoped for it, wanted someone to rescue us from Spooky House and from our weekly dinners at Wendy's, when we sat alongside the hordes of elderly couples squeezing out each other's ketchup. I didn't want to be the only person he depended on. But my father was old, with glasses and high-water corduroys, and I'd thought, *Who would go out with him?*

Sylvia. She was in the bathroom when I returned to my father's room; finally I was alone with him. "Psychic Network?" I asked. "Tarot cards?"

He shrugged. "Personally, at first I thought it was a crock of shit. But she's good at it, you know. She has ESP. She knows who's gonna call before she picks up the phone, and once at her apartment we couldn't find a missing casserole dish, and she sat down and thought about it, then opened the top cabinet and there it was." He sounded sincerely impressed. "I really like Sylvia. We can talk to each other."

I grunted.

"She's picking me up tomorrow, when they release me."

"What time? She doesn't have to–I can leave school early and get you."

"No, she'll do it. But we were thinking that afterward we could all go out to eat," he said.

Sylvia returned from the bathroom then, carrying a cup of water. She was tiny, and my father and I towered over her; I stared at the long white part running through her hair. She removed a vial from her pocketbook and squeezed two droplets into her glass. "I brew my own herbal tinctures in the closet at home," she explained.

How would I survive this dinner? "Can I invite Kelsey?"

My father looked toward Sylvia. "Well, there'll already be four of us . . ."

"Four?"

"Felix is coming too," he said. "Sylvia's son."

"Felix," I told Kelsey. "Felix Feinstein. He's probably three feet tall. He probably has warts. I bet she didn't give birth to him; she brewed him up from a tincture."

"Oh, come on. Stop being so harsh. You never know–he could be cute. The whole thing is kind of touching–like the Brady Bunch."

"Yeah. The Brady Bunch on crack."

"Hey, could you get her to tell me my fortune sometime?" she asked.

"What do you want me to do, rent her out at parties?"

She sighed. "You're so pessimistic. It could work out. Then you wouldn't be complaining about your father all the time."

"Don't even say that. What if it does and Sylvia moves in with us or something, God forbid? Where would all her tinctures go?" I pictured her sitting in our kitchen, miraculously recovering all our missing flatware and cutlery.

"Hey, if nothing else, at least your father's getting some. That's more than we can say for ourselves."

"Thank you for that lovely image," I groaned, and we said good night.

Women who care for their husbands their whole lives always die first.

I'd copied that into my journal right after my mother had said it, her fourth night in the hospital. Underneath that I'd scribbled a guideline to my future self: *Never marry.*

What had she meant, exactly? My mother had given up Rolf and all those other boyfriends, waiting to marry my father until she was thirty-two. And the year after they'd married, he'd had his first heart attack. After all the time I'd spent in the hospital with him, I could see how draining it was to care for him–she'd spent her life doing that.

The upsetting fact was that her death had changed him for the better. She'd complained he wasn't open or affectionate enough before, and now he was. He'd placed framed, enlarged photos of my mom all over the house, made faithful weekly trips to her gravesite, and spoke openly of how he loved her. And now he wanted to go out, he wanted to talk, but with Sylvia. My mother had never gotten to all the possible futures she'd imagined, yet now here was my father, embarking on a new one. Maybe he'd learned from his mistakes, but Sylvia would get the benefit of that.

It couldn't work out with him and Sylvia; it wouldn't be fair. The past shouldn't allow it.

Dinner was at Dreamfood in the East Village, at five o'clock. When I arrived ten minutes late Sylvia and my father had already started in on an appetizer of braised tofu.

"Sorry we began without you. It's my hypoglycemia," Sylvia said. "If I get too hungry, I feel like I'm gonna croak."

I stared at her outfit, a turquoise velour pantsuit lined with purple.

"It's reversible," she said proudly, her eyebrows raised at this ingenuity.

She was extolling the virtues of the Home Shopping Network when Felix walked in. Sylvia had said he was eighteen, but he looked older; he was over six feet tall and tan, with brown hair and blue eyes, and wore a dark gray suit. Normally such an appearance would have an effect on me, but I hardly glanced up from my tofu as we were introduced. I wanted little to do with the Feinstein family.

"Felix had an interview with a *Vogue* photographer today," Sylvia said as he placed a large portfolio against the wall. "For an internship. He's studying to be a fashion photographer. And he's not even gay!"

Felix laughed and planted a kiss on her cheek.

A fashion photographer. I wondered what he thought of reversible pantsuits. "You two don't even look alike," I mumbled, and thought, *Lucky for him.*

Sylvia held her son's hand. "Felix is my only son."

"From her third marriage," my father explained.

Oh, God.

"Henry passed away from a tumor two years ago," Sylvia said.

"I'm sorry," I said. The saga of my family was falling even more unnervingly into depths of TV-movieness. Felix could certainly be the star actor: he swigged his wheatgrass juice as if it was chardonnay, and seemed enthralled by my father's detailed descriptions of defibrillation, and by my father's theory that the hospital cafeteria's chicken was really reconstituted breast implants.

And Felix kept asking about me. I didn't have much to tell. "I'm a sophomore in high school," I said, thinking that was a depressing enough statement in itself to quiet everybody.

"Your father says you do particularly well in English," Felix said.

"Yeah, whatever." What did he care? I wasn't going to be sucked in by this pseudo-interest.

The conversation continued around me: allergies, ailments, medications, shark cartilage, cooking methods for tempeh, the fat content of texturized vegetable protein, a *Health Now* article called "Cheese: The Silent Killer." After a shared slice of carob pie, my father hinted at whether I'd be staying at Kelsey's tonight.

"Not on a school night," I said with horror.

"I forgot it was," he said sheepishly. I knew he wanted to stay at Sylvia's, but I wasn't going to let it happen.

"You could get me a taxi," I said, knowing he wouldn't pay

for one in a million years. "I'll get *killed* if I take the subway at this hour. Especially wearing this short skirt."

My father slouched in his chair, considering the dilemma.

"I'll get her a taxi," Felix interrupted. "I have to go over to Third anyway–there are tons of taxis that way."

It was odd being spoken of as a commodity, a package of loose goods being bargained over. And what did Felix want from me? Why was he being so nice? I wondered if Sylvia had paid him.

She quickly downed her decaf with herbal tincture, and before I could think of any other excuse for why my father had to take me home, he and Sylvia had their coats on and were ready to leave.

"Have a good time!" Sylvia said, and my father didn't even look back as they walked away.

"Do you know, I'm still hungry," Felix said when they were out of sight.

My stomach grumbled slightly too. "Soy isn't very sustaining."

He smiled. "It wasn't bad. But you know what I really want? A sundae. With chocolate fudge and *real* chocolate ice cream. Would you want to share one?"

I wondered if Sylvia and my father had given him a handbook to all my weaknesses. But why not share one with him? I deserved some reward for enduring the evening.

We went to the Village Ice Cream Shoppe and ordered the biggest sundae they had. Gobs of ice cream, fudge, a Belgian waffle, and a thick rich brownie, with sliced bananas and caramel all over it. Ecstasy. Heaven. Orgasmic, Kelsey would say, though eating was as close to orgasming as either of us had ever come.

A half hour later we'd barely made a dent in the mountain of it, but Felix put his spoon down. "Actually, I had another motive for bringing you here. It's rare–it's nice–to talk to someone else who's had a parent who's died."

"Yeah, the Dead Parents Club," I said. "We should get T-shirts."

"Are you always so sarcastic?"

"No."

"I know it's not easy watching your father with another woman. But don't you want him to be happy?"

"Yes," I said indignantly, and we ate the rest of the sundae in silence. I did want my father to be happy. Sometimes I felt wronged by him–exactly for what, I wasn't sure. For not loving my mother enough, or for her death? I couldn't escape that deep inside me I felt, in some essential way, that he should've prevented her death. Or perhaps it was her death that had wronged me, and he was the only one available to blame. But I loved him too–the last two days when he was in the hospital, I'd walked by Wendy's on my way to the subway with a pit in my stomach, missing him. I missed the quiet hum of his television programs, his daily summations of the *New York Times*, even his treatises on the perils of wearing miniskirts on the subway. I was dependent on his company, on his conversation, on *him*, as much–or perhaps even more– than he was on me.

And he had loved my mother, I knew he did. I knew it like the sun comes up, like breathing. I remembered when I was ten, Lucy Gluckman came over and we looked through my parents' drawers. (We'd already done it at her house, uncovering, among other things, a copy of *The Joy of Sex* and an X-rated movie we viewed for thirty horrified minutes.) In my mother's drawer we found a diaphragm. "Ewww!" Lucy had cried, but when I shut the drawer I couldn't help but feel relief, some odd kind of proof of my parents' love.

It was just that there was still so much I didn't comprehend. Like why was I sitting here with Felix right now? Because it wasn't only the sundae that had drawn me here. A part of me wanted something to happen, to be seduced like the women in my books.

My days were filled with crushes and fantasies. And yet, despite all that Kelsey and I read about eternal love and passionate sex in our romance novels, neither of us had any inkling of it in reality.

But I had plenty in my dreams—in my dreams I was a slut. I dreamed of sex with Matthew Broderick, Rob Lowe, Mr. Waller (my math teacher), Steve Madrosian (in my gym class) . . . Sometimes even in the middle of homeroom my mind would go off and undress security guards, the grocer, men I'd seen on the subway, firemen waving from their red trucks. I kept running scenarios, dramas, sexual soap operas continuing each day in class:

Matt Dillon meets me at our high school. He's come to talk to the drama class, he knows someone who knows someone who knows Mr. Klein, the drama teacher. I'm the only girl in the class who doesn't fawn over him—I'm sensible, keeping my distance and playing it perfectly cool. (This was a dream.) He

likes this. Afterward, the other students leave, and even Mr.
Klein has to go. We talk and he kisses me and takes my dress
off, and we make love on Mr. Klein's desk. It hurts at first, but
then it feels wonderful. He kisses my body all over. I've got
chalk on my back. . . .

I wanted to be with a guy, to be lost in him the way I lost myself in books. I imagined that sex would be like that—that it would take away the world, and that afterward there'd be a sense of accomplishment, of having grown older.

The sundae was nearly gone; I stared into the empty bowl.

"I think my father wanted my mother to go out with other men after he died. I know he did. She'd be worse off staying home all alone," Felix said.

I considered filling him in on the box-of-condoms situation but resisted. I shook my head. "My father's too old—it'll give him another heart attack."

"It's not like when you're older you suddenly lose your passion or ability to love."

"Well, Alfred Lord Tennyson, how do you know that?"

"My mother's been married three times."

"Another reason for them not to. She has bad luck."

"She has good luck—it was my father who didn't. It took him a year to die. Every day he suffered, in pain."

I played with my spoon in the empty bowl. "My mother died in twelve days. I don't know if I could've taken it if the dying went on so long."

"I think whatever happens you just somehow take it."

I had to admit, it was good to talk about all this with

someone who'd experienced it too. I wondered if his father's death had made him as crazy as my mother's had made me. Sometimes, lately, I felt a sense of recklessness, of being ready to cast off my cares (and my virginity) in a blink. I thought of the countless times I'd cried in the past ten months, the classes I'd failed. How I still carried the image of my mother everywhere, how I thought she was watching me, all the time, from a corner in the room. Perhaps there she was, by the doorway, even now. Watching us.

The ice cream shop was closing up. "I took photographs of it, when he was dying," he said. "I think that helped me get through it, as some kind of release."

"I kept a journal," I said. "I wrote in it every night." I glanced at his portfolio, resting against the wall. I wanted to see his father's picture; I wanted to know what he looked like. "Could I see your photos?"

"There are only fashion ones in there. The rest are back at my place. My apartment's only three blocks away—do you want to come see them?"

Felix lived above Big Boy's Leather on St. Mark's Place, in a third-floor walk-up. "My roommate's out all night," he explained as he unlocked the door. "He's an insomniac, a painter. He works the night shift at the Kiev."

Their apartment was railroad style, a thin corridor of rooms. It was the messiest place I'd ever seen. You couldn't even see the floor. He draped his suit jacket over a chin-up bar in the doorway to his room. With one fell swoop he cleared two feet of clothes off the couch so I could sit down. The whole room smelled like skunk.

He made coffee in the kitchen. "Instant okay?"

"Sure."

He locked the front door with a loud click. Maybe he would deflower me right there on the couch. That would be an interesting story to tell. *Hey, Kelsey, Felix found his way into my furry domain.* And there I'd be, queen of the schoolyard that day, telling everybody what it was like to no longer be a virgin.

But he didn't make any moves—he took out a folder from the depths of his closet. "I haven't looked at these in a long time," he said, almost nervously.

He sat down on the couch beside me and opened the folder. There were pictures of street people, classmates, several pages of a naked, booberific girl that he quickly flipped through, some of Sylvia, and then his father, the IV, his sickly gray skin.

"I haven't seen these in so long," he said again.

I couldn't stop staring at it: the pain in his father's eyes, his boniness. He looked like a concentration camp victim. In other pictures his body was puffy, like a cartoon.

"The worst was just watching him deteriorate. Bloat up like a balloon from the medication. God, in the end I couldn't even recognize him."

He turned the page. "We had the whole bed, the IV, everything set up in the living room. The house looked like a hospital."

We came to the last photograph—his father's body deflated, like a rag doll, a skeleton with soft bones. It was then that

Felix's voice cracked and he started to cry. I couldn't believe it; I'd never seen a young guy cry, except in anger.

"I'm sorry I brought you up here," he said, his voice quavering. "I didn't do it planning to look like an idiot . . ."

I put my hand over his. It happened naturally; I touched him without my even willing it. I waited patiently while he cried, relieved not to be the one sobbing, for a change. When the tears stopped he squeezed my hand tighter, bent toward it, and kissed my fingers. Then he kissed me.

His hand ran up my calf, to my knee, under my skirt. (What underwear did I have on? Oh, good, the nice pink ones.) Along the outside of my sweater, to my neck, he kissed my neck, his hands back over my sweater, right across my breasts. Not a slip of the hand; he was unabashedly touching my breasts.

I didn't want him to stop. I arched toward him as he slipped his hand beneath my sweater's trim.

"I want you," Felix said.

I wished he hadn't said that, because all I could think of right then was my mother again, watching us, laughing her head off. Maybe she'd be up there with Henry, Felix's father, the two of them shaking their heads.

"I want you," he said again.

Or maybe not. More likely they had better things to do. My mother was up there somewhere with her aunts and cousins, getting her hair and nails done at the great salon in the sky.

"I want you."

How could she not be laughing? I'd told her once, long before she got sick, that I'd wait till I met someone I loved to have sex. There was no rush, I told her. I wanted it to be real. And she was pleased to hear it. *You have a lot of sense,* she had said. *You already know something about love.*

His fingers reached into my underpants. He was playing with the edges, the bikini elastic. His fingers reached down and lingered between my legs.

For a moment it felt so good I thought I was going to die.

Then he started pushing his fingers inside of me. Reaching one, then two; I squirmed. He took this as a good sign, and dug deeper, like he was urgently searching for something. *What, did you lose something in there? A fingernail? A ring?*

He kept on digging, and I kept squirming until finally I grabbed his wrist, his fingers slid out of me, and I said, "I have to go."

He lay still, searching me with his eyes. "I don't want you to go."

Maybe it was a mistake to leave. Maybe I'd never get the chance to have sex again. Maybe I'd get hit by a bus on the way home, or stabbed by a drug dealer, or diagnosed with cancer and die in twelve days.

Or maybe my mother wasn't watching me after all–I was just watching myself.

"I have to go," I said again. I straightened my clothes.

"Come on–you can stay. We won't do anything, I promise–"

"I need to go. I'll–I'll see you." I put on my coat and left his apartment. I reached my arm out for a taxi, and I went home.

"You're lucky you didn't have sex with him," Kelsey said. "Can you imagine? What if you got pregnant? Then no matter what happens with your father, you'd be *related* to Sylvia."

We were upstairs in my bedroom; downstairs Sylvia was cooking lentils for dinner. "The way things look, it seems like I'll be related to her no matter what," I said. "My father's been seeing her almost every night." He'd been home from the hospital a little over a week, and I told Kelsey how the night before, while he was out with Sylvia, I'd snuck into his bathroom and peeked inside his toilet kit again. The condom box was still there. I'd opened it, tensing my shoulders—it was empty.

"It's gross, really gross," I told Kelsey. "There were twelve condoms in that box. *Twelve.*"

"That must be one hell of a pacemaker he's got."

"Or one of Sylvia's tinctures."

All throughout dinner Kelsey and I stared at Sylvia and my father, searching for clues to their libidos. We ate the lentil casserole ("*Maybe it's the lentils,*" Kelsey whispered) while Sylvia told us Felix had gotten the *Vogue* internship and was in Antarctica photographing models on ice floes.

"Great," I said. "He must be happy."

"Imagine him with all those gorgeous models!"

I forced a smile, and Kelsey asked Sylvia if she would read our tarot cards. She agreed to, and after dinner we began.

She read Kelsey's cards first, revealing the Empress, a woman holding a wand that resembled an ice cream cone—it meant future success, Sylvia said—and the Knight of Wands, the King of Cups, lots of handsome, lusty-looking men, even one who oddly resembled Matt Dillon. All guaranteed good fortune in some form or another. Kelsey beamed.

Then Sylvia read mine. She laid them out on the coffee table, the colorful array. In the center of it all was a picture of a red heart with huge swords stabbing through it.

"Oh, figures," I said. "Story of my life."

But Sylvia said no. She said one card is never all that we are.

Cures for

Heartbreak

depressing business, heartbreak, no picnic no matter how you look at it. But never fear, you can cure yourself if you feel like it. Follow these handy instructions.

—Cynthia Heimel
Sex Tips for Girls

THE NAPKINS WERE the wrong shade of lilac. "It's not exactly lilac, is the problem here," my father was saying on the phone to Denny of Denny's Discount Party Rentals. "My fiancée, she's a little nuts. Everything has to match. . . . You're telling me. Okay, it has sort of a shimmer–no, *shimmer's* the wrong word. It's–what do you call it? When it's multicolored in different lights, almost like a rainbow? Like a dragonfly wing?"

"Iridescent," I shouted from the dining room table, where piles of iridescent lilac invitation components were spread before us.

"Don't help him," Alex said.

I shrugged.

"Batshit. He's gone completely batshit," she mumbled.

"It's the psychic's fault," I said. Sylvia had splurged on a visit to a fancy psychic-to-the-stars after my father had asked her to marry him. *Elizabeth Taylor sees her all the time,* Sylvia had told us with pride. The psychic had informed Sylvia that she "needed to do it right and have a proper fête" this time, for what would be her fourth marriage.

Our father had asked Sylvia to marry him on Valentine's Day at their favorite eatery, Dreamfood. After a mouthwatering repast of bulgur cassoulet and yucca quiche, Harold, my father's favorite waiter, brought out the leatherette bill folder. Tucked inside was a note: WILL YOU MARRY ME? My father had typed it at home on the Smith Corona.

My father was telling Denny the story.

"I had Harold put the ring inside that pocket doohickey where the credit card goes."

Alex rolled her eyes.

"Best part was, the meal was on the house! . . . Thank you . . . I know, it's not a common color. What can you do? . . . Thanks for your help! . . . You too."

He hung up the phone. "Guess I'll be hemming the napkins myself."

Hemming them? When my father sold his shop, he'd sworn he'd never stitch another thing again. We still had his mother's old Singer sewing machine, but he hadn't used it since he sewed my Snoopy costume in fifth grade.

"If Sylvia wants matching napkins, then *she* should sew them." Alex shook her head. "Or use paper ones. This whole thing is crazy. You've only known her five months."

My father shrugged. "When you know, you know."

"It could be worse," I told my sister. "We could be heading off to Vegas–that's where she eloped last time." I pictured my father in a sequined suit, being married at a drive-through chapel.

"Her other two weddings were at City Hall," my father said. "She never even had a wedding dress! She wore the same

180

cream suit to the last three. This time she'll have a lovely dress, and our families will be there, our friends, a rabbi, and maybe a live musician or two."

Our parents had gotten married at the Parker North, a small hotel in upper Manhattan that no longer existed. Our mother had worn a short white sixties dress that now lay in a box on the top shelf of my closet. In the pictures my father had a full head of hair and a huge bohemian daisy in his pocket. Not an iridescent lilac in sight. She'd been dead a year and three months now.

My father turned to me. "Do you still have that xylophone?"

"What?"

"Maybe, for the procession, you could play–"

"You want me to bang out Pachelbel's Canon on the xylophone?"

"You wouldn't believe what these harpists charge."

Alex grumbled something unintelligible under her breath.

"What did you say?" my father asked her. "Catshit?"

She shook her head.

"Girls, please don't kvetch. I need your help."

"We *are* helping," Alex said. "Look." She pointed at the stack of finished envelopes that we'd hand-addressed for their July wedding. Our father had asked us to address them after boasting about our penmanship to Sylvia.

The invitations had been ordered off the Forever Yours catalog and featured two intertwined silver hearts on ivory paper with lilac trim. Alex picked up her calligraphy pen and started writing out an address. "We're almost done. Who the hell is Prina Norval, anyway?" she asked our father.

"I don't know. Someone from Sylvia's side. Wait. I forgot, I have a couple more pages of addresses too." He disappeared upstairs to fetch them.

"Had I known this was how I was going to be spending my spring break, I would've stayed at school," Alex said. She stamped the return address with the rubber stamp our father ordered that said "Pearlman Palace" above our address. He thought that was quite funny.

"You would do that to me? Leave me here to deal with this all alone?" I asked.

"The whole thing just galls me. Mommy's only been dead a little over a year."

"I've heard of worse. A guy Kelsey's brother knows, his dad remarried four months after their mother died."

She shook her head.

"At least she's not moving in," I said, glancing around the living room. "Thank God." Sylvia refused to give up her apartment in Manhattan on West 90th Street, so they were going to keep their separate homes. As long as I was okay with it (I was) he'd spend a couple of nights a week in Manhattan with her, and she'd spend weekends in Queens at her new "country home." Unfortunately, her presence had materialized on a few weeknights as well. She was coming over this afternoon, a Friday–I was on spring break too–for lunch.

Our father returned with three new pages of scrawled names and addresses.

Alex glanced at them. "Morty Grossman? Why does that name sound familiar?"

It took me a second and then I remembered. I grabbed the

list. Cindy and Alva Curry. Gina Petrollo. Richard Bridgewald, Gigi and Sasha Backus, Shelly Petra.

My mouth opened in horror. "You're inviting people from the hospital and Green Springs? *Why?*"

"They're friends," he said.

"They're not friends! You never saw them again!"

"I'd like to invite them," he said.

Alex smiled brightly. "We can give nitroglycerin tablets as favors."

"Whatever you do, you're not inviting that crazy social worker. No way." I swiped the black calligraphy marker across Gina Petrollo's name, and then did the same through Richard Bridgewald's underneath it.

"How'd you get all their addresses?" Alex asked.

He shrugged. "The sheet from Green Springs had everybody there on it . . . and Morty and the others I looked up in the phone book. Sylvia said we needed to invite more people. She wants a big wedding." He glanced at the clock. "Shit. She's going to be here any minute. I've got to start lunch—eggless egg salad okay with you girls?"

"Fine," I said.

"Delicious," Alex said.

I picked up an envelope and wrote Gigi and Sasha's address, *800 Degraw Street, Brooklyn, New York,* in my best handwriting. I pointed to Sasha's name. "That's the cancer guy," I whispered to my sister.

"No."

"Yup. He lived."

She squinted. "Who else is he going to invite? Rabbi Elvis?"

"Shh. Don't give him any ideas."

I stuffed the envelope and put it on the stack. I couldn't believe that it would go to Gigi and Sasha's house. "I'm sure they won't come," I said.

"Let's hope not."

"What if no one shows up? Can you imagine?" I asked.

"Please. I'm praying no one shows up. It's going to be humiliating."

I nodded and drew a swirl around the y in Alva Curry's name.

Our father turned on the kitchen radio to the country music station. A woman twanged about her heart being trampled into one million pieces–*one million pieces*, the chorus went, *one million pieces, one million pieces.* A few minutes later Sylvia walked through the door, out of breath.

"I spent the whole morning registering!" She wore a fuchsia trench coat and eyeglasses that darkened in the light. Indoors, the lenses were the color of a thunderhead.

"He let her register by herself? Oh, God," I whispered. I could only imagine what she'd registered for. I gazed around the living room at the flourishes she'd added to our house since she'd become engaged to our father–the green-flowered valances that now perched atop our windows, the chintz cushions daintily aligned on our plain brown sofa, looking like princesses who'd sat down in the wrong place. She'd packed our fridge with herbal tinctures. Then, two weeks ago, she'd brought over her beloved Zingy-Dell Collectible Figurines and housed them in a cabinet in our hallway. I'd never heard of Zingy-Dell figurines before, and neither had my father nor Alex, though according to Sylvia they were extremely popular. "What a load of crap," my father said (out of earshot of Sylvia) when he finished assembling the authentic Zingy-Dell cabinet she'd special-ordered. The Zingy-Dell figurines featured puffy-cheeked children, bears, and bunnies smiling on pedestals in honor of such occasions as birthdays and Valentine's Day; others dispensed general advice such as "Smiles" (a bunny with a toothy grin), "Just Sunshine" (a special limited-edition bear clutching a sun), and "Keep on Truckin'" (puffy child in a tow truck). Each came with a Guaranteed Certificate of Authenticity. "Because you wouldn't want a fake Zingy-Dell," Alex said. "God forbid."

We all knew what was coming from the registry: there was plenty of empty space in that cabinet.

"Why not select a charity and have people donate to that as wedding gifts—like the American Cancer Society?" I suggested. We'd once gone to a wedding for one of my mother's co-workers who had done that.

"Good idea. Maybe we'll do that too," Sylvia said. "But I hear lots of people like to give something more concrete."

"Eh, who's really going to buy us gifts?" my dad said. "We don't *need* anything."

"There's lots we need! I saw some lovely crystal decanters at Fortunoff. And dessert bowls. And a chandelier. Plus you wouldn't believe the selection at Harry's Collectibles. They gave me these cards we can put in with the invitations announcing the registries." She handed one to us. *Sylvia Feinstein and Simon Pearlman are pleased to announce their wedding registry at Harry's Collectibles.*

"We sealed most of the invitations already," Alex said.

"Maybe you can call them and spread the word, then." She handed a similar card to us from Fortunoff.

We sat down to the eggless egg salad.

"Hold on, I almost forgot." She picked up her pocketbook and withdrew two pink envelopes. "Before we start eating–these are for you."

She handed one envelope to me and one to Alex.

"Thank you," I said. What was it? A Harry's Collectibles gift certificate? I opened the card.

Among a field of purple flowers swam the words: *Will you be my bridesmaid?*

"Oh," I said. "Wow."

Alex kept staring at her matching card, as if it was in a foreign language.

My father looked proud. He'd clearly known this was coming. "Girls?" he asked, waiting.

"Great. Great! I'm–we're–honored," I stuttered, not knowing what else to say.

Sylvia beamed. "I can't wait to show you the material for your dresses! Your father has so graciously offered to sew them. Simon, you didn't show them the fabric yet, did you? Did you spoil the surprise?" She rummaged through a bag in the closet and came out with–of course–a bolt of lilac iridescent cloth. She stroked the material. "Real silk! Felix got it for us at a discount. Isn't it snazzy?"

"Snazzy," Alex said.

My father pinched the fabric between his fingers. "I hope there's enough for the napkins, too. I've been calling everywhere and none of the shops have that color."

186

"There'll be plenty left over. Enough for a souvenir table-cloth too! Or curtains! Girls, it means so much to me that you're doing this." She hugged us, her bony elbow poking into my arm. "You know, your father asked Felix to be his best man."

"No, I didn't know. Really?" My stomach twisted. In a shadowy corner of my mind, memories of my night with Felix peeked through—his lips on mine, his fingers. *Ugh.* What had I been thinking? Kelsey called him the Boy Whose Fingers Have Gone Where No Fingers Have Gone Before. It was disturbing on a staggering number of levels that my father's best man would be someone I'd made out with and, even worse, would soon be *related* to. I'd never told Alex nor my father what we'd done; I hoped if I stopped thinking about it, it would just go away. After all, Felix seemed to have the same attitude. The couple of times we'd seen each other since, he'd ignored me. He was probably just as embarrassed as I was.

Our father partly unrolled the bolt and held the fabric beneath our faces. "You're going to look stunning." His voice cracked.

"Mia, sweetie, is that you?" a woman said on the phone Saturday morning. I squinted at my clock: a little after nine.

"Huh?"

"I'm sorry to call so early! I came home late last night and got the invitation, and I couldn't wait to congratulate your dad! I'm so happy to hear he's doing so well. It was so kind of him to invite us."

"Yeah." Who are you?

"Sasha and I will definitely come. We'd love to. It was just so thoughtful of your family to invite us. I love weddings. I love happy endings."

I sat up.

"In fact, I wanted to invite you and your sister and your dad and his fiancée to dinner here next Sunday. To celebrate how good things have turned out. Sasha's home and he'd love to see all of you too."

"How is he?"

"Good! Really good! He took this crazy trip. Oh my God. He's got pictures. He's got slides. We've got slides coming out of our assholes. Pardon my French. We'll show you all of them when you come for dinner. May I talk to your dad?"

"Sure. I'll go get him." I went to his room and woke him up. He was alone; Sylvia was visiting her mother in New Jersey.

"Gigi Backus is on the phone."

He blinked and nodded and picked up the receiver. I opened the curtains and stared out at the street while he told Gigi about Sylvia. "Great. We'll see you Sunday," he said. "What can we bring? . . . Ha! Not that!"

"What?" I asked when he'd hung up.

"The kidney dish."

That was the blue crescent-shaped tray they gave people to barf into at NYU Medical Center.

"Just a little hospital humor," my father said, still chuckling.

⌒◌ ◌⌒

The next Sunday I helped my sister pack to go back to school. "I hope you have a fun dinner with the cancer guy tonight," she said as she crammed her clean laundry into her monster-sized backpack.

"I'll try."

"Maybe while I'm away you can accidentally spill something on the purple putridescent fabric? Or run it through the paper shredder?"

"I'll see what I can do. I get the feeling Sylvia has access to an endless supply of it, though."

I touched her backpack. I was suddenly feeling needy for her, wanting her to stay, not wanting to be left with our father and Sylvia. Our *stepmother,* almost—I couldn't get used to that word. *My father's girlfriend,* I called her. *My father's soon-to-be wife.* I kept telling myself to be mature about the whole thing. We'd moved my mother's clothes from her closet into mine and Alex's now-empty one. ("You're being very adult about this," my dad had complimented me after the engagement. Which had made me feel guilty about the doodle I'd drawn on the inside back cover of my school-owned *Tale of Two Cities:* a green Sylvia with hairy warts.)

"He seems happier, though, right? I mean, you didn't see him when he was on the couch all the time, reading the *New York Times* all day long. It was depressing," I said.

She shrugged. I knew she felt he was being disloyal to our mother, no matter what, that he was breaking an unwritten code by getting married again, and it was possible that she might never forgive him. It was weakness, she believed, to buckle to the need for a new marriage, to not be able to be alone. I could tell from her accusing gazes and glances at him, her unwavering annoyance–it all condemned his disloyalty. I was glad she was so vehement; it took some of the pressure off me. She was our steadfast conscience.

"I'll miss you," I said.

"Really?"

"Yup. You're lucky you don't have to stay here." But even as I said it I wasn't sure I was ready to leave.

"You only have two and a half more years before you go to college."

I shrugged, helped her pack the rest of her things, and then walked her to the subway. She was taking the 7 train to the Port Authority, since our father and Sylvia had driven to Briar Manor in Westchester that afternoon to meet with the wedding planner.

We walked quietly along the three blocks to the station together, past Cardially Yours Cards & Gifts, TemTee Foods, the Merry-Go-Round Gentlemen's Club, Tony's Meat Market, and Sunny Grocery, the storefronts we'd known all our lives.

At the subway station she adjusted her backpack on her shoulders. "I'll come down for the weekend soon. Good luck here. Keep on truckin'." We hugged, and she left.

My father and Sylvia picked me up three hours later to drive to Gigi and Sasha's in Brooklyn. They were glowing from their visit to Briar Manor. My father wore a new corduroy blazer and jeans with suspenders; Sylvia was in a green tunic and matching pants. I climbed into the backseat.

"You wouldn't believe this Briar Manor," he told me. "It's a beauty-full property."

"*Beautiful,*" I corrected. "Not *beauty-full.*"

He ignored me. "They have a pond with ducks! We saw two ducks screwing."

"Yes, they were fornicating," Sylvia said.

Who were these people? I gazed out the window to the Brooklyn-Queens Expressway. They were going to mortify me at this dinner. I'd primped for it–I wore black knee-high boots and a maroon miniskirt, and had spent a half hour applying makeup. My fingers clenched on my pocketbook, then relaxed. The whole cancer guy crush had been an episode of girlish stupidity. I knew that. I'd grown beyond such things now. The next time I liked someone, it wouldn't be a crush, it would be real–and it would turn into an actual boyfriend-girlfriend thing. That's what I'd decided. Seeing the cancer guy tonight–so what? So what.

We got off at the Atlantic Avenue exit. Their neighborhood was five minutes away, two blocks from the projects.

"Keep your door locked," Sylvia said as my father searched for a parking spot. We had no trouble finding one. "Simon, use the Club," she warned him.

I got out of the car and stared up at their long brownstone stoop. It was nothing like I'd imagined. I'd pictured them living in a house just like the boxy brick ones we had in Queens, with white cement trim or plastic awnings. Instead I peered up at their stately brownstone, its intricate moldings, its imposing front door. We rang the bell, and Gigi bounded downstairs to greet us.

"Don't you look gorgeous!" She hugged me. "My God! And Simon! And you must be Sylvia! I'm so glad you could come. What a wonderful thing. I'm so happy for you." She hugged them too and led us upstairs; their apartment was on the top two stories. It had pine plank floors, a fireplace, and huge long skinny windows. There were rainbow decals on the windows, rainbow switchplates on the walls, and a rainbow wind chime by the door. A gray cat was sprawled on the couch, asleep. Sylvia sneezed.

Hovering by a tall wooden bookcase was Sasha.

I hardly recognized him. His hair had grown black and long, to his cheekbones. He was tanned and still thin, not tall, but stronger-looking. Healthy.

"Hi," he said.

"Hi," I said.

"Sasha, you remember Mia and Simon, of course, and this is Sylvia!" Gigi crooned.

"Nice to meet you." He shook Sylvia's hand.

"Here, don't be shy," Gigi said, offering us a plate of cheese and crackers.

My father beamed. "Cheese!"

"Oh, no." Sylvia backed away as if cheese spores might be floating through the air and infecting her veins.

"Simon called and told me you were healthy eaters." Gigi smiled and waved her hand. "One bite won't kill you."

Sasha spread a cracker with cheese and offered it to me. I thanked him. Then he made one for my father.

"None for me, thanks." Sylvia positioned herself as far away from the offending hors d'oeuvre as possible.

Gigi brought out wineglasses for everyone, including me. She paused the bottle above my glass with a glance at my father.

"Sure!" he said, and she poured away.

"You look very healthy," Sylvia told Sasha. "Really." She sounded surprised and unconvinced.

"You look good too, Simon, very robust," Gigi told my dad.

"Thank you. I feel very robust." My dad helped himself to another cheese and cracker. "Sasha, I hear you're a world traveler."

Gigi touched Sasha's arm. "Sweetie, can you get the pictures?"

"Sure." Sasha disappeared into another room and brought out a huge cloth-covered album. "The first half is Europe and the second half is Nepal. We have slides too, but I think we'll spare you those." His voice was deep but gentle. Soft.

"Nepal." My dad shook his head in awe.

"He wasn't supposed to go to Nepal. No, that wasn't in the original plan. We agreed he was going to keep traveling an extra two weeks, and then he calls me up. 'Ma, guess where I am?' he says. '*Kathmandu,*' he says. Kathmandu? Aaah!" She pretended to choke him and then kissed his head.

I sipped the wine; it tasted sour, but I pretended to like it. I'd had wine before but preferred it in the form of wine coolers.

"Nepal. That is very daring of you to go there," Sylvia said. "Very, very daring."

We flipped through the album, past Montmartre and Provence and Amsterdam, to pictures of yaks, monkeys, snow-covered glaciers, and tiny villages. Gigi had put the album together; it was her bubbly handwriting and exclamation points beneath the pictures, her *i*'s dotted with circles.

"Weren't you worried?" Sylvia asked.

"Was I worried? I almost died of worry," Gigi said. She turned to Sasha. "Remember, I kept trying to call you in Patan? I asked for Sasha and the manager of the hotel said, 'Dead! Dead!' I practically had a heart attack."

Sylvia gasped. "What did you do?"

"Turned out the guy meant the phone line was going dead–he couldn't hear me."

A timer in the kitchen rang. "That's the lasagna. Why don't we move to the table? I want to hear all about your wedding plans," Gigi said.

Sasha refilled my father's wineglass, then his own.

"I want to do it right this time, I really do," Sylvia said. "That's why we're going to have the whole big shebang."

"I just love weddings. I hope Sasha has a big wedding someday."

"Mom."

"I know, I know, you probably want to get married in Kathmandu on top of a yak. Just let me help pick out the flowers, okay? Or at least the color of the yak."

Everyone laughed. "Colored yaks! That's what we need for our wedding," my father said. "Of course they have to be iridescent lilac."

"Lilacs—is that the flower you picked for your bouquet?" Gigi asked as we sat down at the dining room table.

"Fresh ones for the centerpieces, but silk ones for my bouquet because I'm allergic."

"I made this with whole-wheat noodles. Simon told me you're allergic to white flour. And I used low-fat ricotta."

"Yes, thank you, smells wonderful," Sylvia trilled.

Gigi served the lasagna and salad. She stared at my father and Sasha as we passed dishes down the table. "Seems like ages ago that we met you. Sasha took his turn for the better after that—his second remission, and his counts are great!" She plopped a gargantuan lettuce leaf onto a plate. "We are so lucky."

"We're all lucky," Sylvia said. "I don't know if Simon told you, but I'm a lung cancer survivor myself." She launched into the details of her treatments, how the cancer had spread to her lymph nodes but she was doing just fine, just great, how she was participating in a clinical trial of a new drug that seemed incredibly promising. I knew all this, and if I'd been a better person it would have given me great sympathy for her and an enlarged capacity for kindness. But it irritated me. It annoyed me that she should live for so many years with this advanced cancer when my mother had died in twelve days. It bothered me that her own mother was still alive. If Sylvia had not been so diametrically different a person from my mother, with her herbal tinctures and tarot cards and Zingy-Dell figurines, if she'd been normal, then I would've liked her. Or so I told myself.

Sasha shoveled in his lasagna. I was sitting next to him and kept glancing at him as Sylvia recounted her litany of health woes. He had dark brown hairs on his forearms; his hands were strong and wide as he gripped his water glass.

His eyes were a color I couldn't quite name. Seafoam. Aquamarine. Topaz. These were the colors from the Forever Yours wedding supplies catalog, which had implanted themselves in my brain. There was something mischievous about his face, its angles and long dimples—had those dimples been there before? His smile was alarming. Warm and direct, it caught me off guard; I almost felt he could see what I was thinking.

I wanted to touch him. I found myself almost involuntarily edging my thigh closer until it brushed his jeans.

"Sasha's going to start at Columbia this fall," Gigi said.

"Really? What's your major going to be?" Sylvia pushed the ricotta filling to the side of her plate.

"I'm not sure yet. Philosophy, maybe."

"He's always reading that stuff. Kant, Kierkegaard, Heidegger . . . What's that thing you were talking about the other day, honey—*Dasein*?"

"Casein? The milk protein?" Sylvia asked.

"*Dasein*. It's a concept of being," Sasha said.

Sylvia stuffed a huge piece of lettuce into her mouth. "Philosophy. Not a lot of jobs in that!"

"True." He grinned politely. He caught me staring at him; I looked away.

The conversation returned to the wedding again, the challenge of finding iridescent lilac everything, the vegetarian menu, the fat-free cake, my dad and Sylvia's plans to honeymoon in Florida.

"We might drive all the way to Key West. Though I hear it's very gay," Sylvia said.

"I'm going to wrestle alligators," my dad said matter-of-factly.

Everyone had finished eating; I got up to help Gigi and Sasha clear the plates.

"Sweetie, why don't you show Mia the view from the roof?" Gigi asked him.

"Sure."

I followed him to the other side of the apartment and up two flights. The dark sky opened around us. From above, the connected brownstones looked so much smaller, so insignificant. We looked out over the brownstone rows and treetops to the glittery Manhattan buildings. "It looks so close from here," I said. "Same in our neighborhood. We can see the Empire State Building from Skillman Avenue, and it looks like it's right there. Or down the tracks of the number seven train— the skyline seems so close you could touch it. I wish we lived there." In my school, being asked *Are you from Manhattan?* was the highest compliment. If someone guessed you were from Queens it meant you had applied too much eyeliner, or styled your hair too big, or bought your clothes at ABC Discount Variety on Queens Boulevard instead of at a chic secondhand shop in the Village.

"I love Queens. Alley Pond Park, Breezy Point, the Rockaways—my mom used to take me there." He smiled. "It's funny, being in another country—people are impressed sometimes when you say you're from New York. They think it's this amazing, exciting place, like in the movies."

197

"That's funny." A siren screamed by. "When we were little we used to beg our parents to move to the country. It seemed so exciting. . . . I wanted to be like Laura Ingalls Wilder or Anne of Green Gables. I mean, the only places I've ever been are Maplewood, upstate, and the Poconos . . . in the Poconos my sister and I used to freak out over seeing all those stars."

I looked up: nothing. You could never see them in the city.

"Virginia," I said. "I've been to Virginia too." I winced, remembering how preoccupied I'd been with my own impending death then, and how I'd been certain of Sasha's. I gazed at my boots.

"Virginia?"

"My dad and I were there for this thing over the summer called Healthy Heart Week. I was his companion—it was pre-Sylvia. We met some interesting southerners—you might see them at the wedding. If you hear anyone use the word *hineybumper* or the phrase *bet your bippy*, that's them." He was easy to talk to, for some reason—he seemed to listen. I didn't feel so nervous being near him now, alone in the dark.

"What's a bippy?"

"Synonym for *hineybumper.* Which is a synonym for *butt.*"

"Good to know." His smile looked sly this time, like we were sharing a secret.

"They're inviting a number of oddities to the wedding. Not you guys, I mean—people like Morty Grossman. Wasn't he in the ICU with you?"

"No. I don't know Morty."

"Right. That was another time. Anyway, my dad met him in the hospital too. I can't believe he's still alive."

Too late, I realized that this was an insulting thing to say. "I'm sorry," I said lamely.

"Why are you sorry?"

"I didn't mean–" I stared at the lit windows of the brownstones across the street and changed the subject. "I crossed off a couple people he was going to invite–oh my God. This crazy social worker–"

"Uh-oh. I hope you're not talking about this one woman they sent me. She was supposed to be the best on the staff, but she was the *worst*." He shook his head and scratched the sleeve of his black sweater.

"Did she have a huge hineybumper?"

He grinned. "She did."

"Gina Petrollo?"

"That's right, that's her name! God, she was nuts." He laughed.

"When my dad was about to have bypass surgery, Miss Petrollo told me to go shopping. Not that it was entirely bad advice, in retrospect, but at the time it didn't seem exactly professional."

"She told me I needed a hobby. She suggested whittling. You know, carving sticks into trinkets?" he asked.

"Lovely."

"I actually sort of like whittling. Still . . ."

"Still."

He dug his hands into the pockets of his jeans and stared

up at the sky. We kept gazing above us for a long time, as if waiting for a star to miraculously show itself. We didn't speak; I wasn't sure if I should say something, if I should ask about his health or about philosophy.

Something about the word *philosophy* made my heart quicken. We had no philosophy classes at my high school–nothing even close. I thought of the class descriptions I'd read in Alex's college course catalog when it came in the mail–I'd nearly salivated at the thickness of the catalog; I'd read it page by page until she forced me to give it back to her. I'd circled some of the classes, dreaming about all the things you could study: *Feminist Philosophy, Knowledge and Power, Women in American Society;* there was even a class called *Cinematic Desire.* It thrilled me that in college you could finally choose what you wanted to learn. The course catalog had seemed like an emblem of the future–there was something to look forward to.

"Philosophy," I said finally. "I might like to study that too."

"This Eastern one I've been reading about, Taoism?" he said, still gazing upward. "They believe that nature is the force of good, and whatever happens in nature always works out right."

"Huh." I'd heard of Taoism–my father had a copy of *The Tao of Pooh,* though I didn't think he'd ever read it. "Maybe that's why I like the country. Maybe I should go trek in Nepal."

"Do you like hiking?"

"I love it." What was I saying? The only place I'd hiked to was Bloomingdale's Shoes on 2.

"I'm going next weekend–I've been taking Metro-North upstate and exploring the trails and mountains there."

"By yourself?"

"Usually I go by myself. Actually, always. You're welcome to come. If you want," he said.

I wanted. "Sure. It sounds fun." What was happening here, exactly?

He stared at my boots with the three-inch heels. "You have hiking boots, right? You need them–it might be icy in some places still."

"Of course I've got hiking boots." I hoped Alex's old ones would fit me with some thick socks.

"We can meet at Grand Central next Saturday, then. At the info booth? There's a train that leaves at eleven–we can catch the sunset before we come back. Meet at ten-thirty to get our tickets?"

"Okay–sounds fun," I said. "Great."

We were silent for a while, until Gigi's voice shrilled from the stairs. "Ya guys fall off? Come on–dessert's ready!"

"We'll be down in a sec," Sasha called. He paused. "No offense, but you're really different than I thought you were. When I met you at NYU I thought you were kind of . . . " He shrugged. "Obnoxious. I mean–you're not at all. I'm just surprised."

Obnoxious?

"Don't look so horrified. I didn't know you or anything."

"Oh, well. Jeez." *Obnoxious?*

"I didn't mean that in a bad way."

I felt a hot wave of shame, remembering our awkward conversation in the solarium almost a year ago. "Yeah. Maybe I was kind of . . . I guess . . . I was sort of, well . . . freaked out by everything, I guess."

" 'Cause of your dad, you mean?"

I shrugged. "Everything."

"NYU?"

NYU—he said it like the university, not the hospital. As if we went to college there together.

"I remember you were talking to me this one time and I was reading this embarrassing book and I didn't want you to see it," I said.

"Why?"

"It was a romance novel. I don't usually read that stuff—I never do—but I didn't want you to see. I thought you'd think I was stupid."

"A romance novel." He smiled.

I felt like he could see straight into my organs in the dark. I regretted telling him.

"I never read them anymore," I lied.

Gigi called from the stairs again. "We're going to eat dessert without you!"

"We're coming!" Sasha yelled. He gently touched my elbow. "We better head down. Saturday. Don't forget," he said.

Throughout dessert and the whole ride home I felt like I was carrying a secret. We didn't mention anything about hiking together after we rejoined the grown-ups, and I didn't tell my dad or Sylvia on the drive home. I wanted to keep it to myself.

"I can't believe she let him go to Nepal. That's *crazy,*"

Sylvia said as we sped along the Brooklyn-Queens Expressway. "He could've caught an infectious disease! His immunity must be very low. If he caught anything, he'd be dead. It's ridiculous, a third-world country. They don't even have medical care there. So *reckless*."

"He was very lucky," my dad said.

"But he was fine," I told them. "He was fine in Nepal. He didn't catch any infectious diseases. He's fine."

She ignored me. "She's obviously very permissive. Serving the kids wine."

"My mom let us taste wine and beer. It was never a big deal," I said. "It didn't lead me to start freebasing in the school hallways or anything."

"It's just not appropriate," Sylvia said to my father, not to me.

I sighed, put on my Walkman, and listened to music for the rest of the drive home. I lay down in the backseat and tuned them out, dreaming about Sasha, replaying our conversation on the roof.

On Monday after school, Kelsey and I went shopping for hiking boots at Paragon Sports. Alex had taken both her pairs to Cornell with her.

"I need to make them look used," I said, picking up a pair of clunky, hideous gray boots. "A hundred dollars? Jesus." I put them back down. "He thinks I'm a hiker. Do you think if I bat a pair against the cement and rub in some dirt they'll look used?"

"Please don't turn into a crazy hiking-boot crunchy person," she said.

"Don't worry. I won't."

"What is it that you like about this guy, anyway?"

"I don't know. He's nice and . . . there's something about him that's so different from other guys. Like he skipped the whole artificial *I'm a boy, I'm cool, I'm angry* thing . . . he's just himself. He's really gentle–his voice, everything. He just seems so . . . nice."

She looked skeptical. "The cancer thing doesn't bother you? I mean, what if he dies?" I'd told her how in Virginia I'd convinced myself that he was dead.

"He looks really healthy and fine. I don't think he's going to keel over on our date, if that's what you're worried about."

"Do you know CPR?"

"No. Should I?"

"Can't hurt."

I pictured his face, his black hair falling in his eyes. "His cancer brings him down to my rung," I said. "It's like an equalizer–he would never be interested in the likes of me if he was healthy."

"You're crazy." She shook her head.

"No, really–he's that cute," I said. "He has this smile . . . with dimples . . . and cheekbones . . ."

She picked up a pair of brown leather boots. "Hiking," she said. "*Why?* What's the point? Can't you just drive up the mountain?"

"I don't think there's a road." I shrugged. "It's supposed to be fun." But I was a little nervous. Shit. What if I had to scale rock faces with my bare hands?

"What are you going to wear?"

"Khaki pants and my black crewneck sweater."

"I think you should just get these." She picked up a pair of maroon sneakers. "They're cute, and they'll work just as well as hiking boots. Hiking boots are fugly. How can you pay so much for something so fugly?"

I examined the maroon sneakers.

"They're seventy dollars cheaper," she said.

That sealed the deal. I bought the sneakers and a pair of wool socks.

"You'd better be careful. I hate the woods. There are axe murderers and stuff out there," she said as we walked to the subway.

"I know. I'll be careful. Hey–can you be my alibi? I'm not telling my dad I'm going. He'd tell Sylvia and she'd say something annoying and I just don't want to get into it."

"Sure. Of course. Just don't let the cancer guy die on you or anything."

Sasha was waiting at the info booth at Grand Central on Saturday. He grinned when he saw me and studied my face.

"You look nice. Are you wearing makeup?"

"Makeup? No! Of course not." I laughed nervously and vowed to be careful when rummaging through my knapsack so he wouldn't see the powder, blush, lipstick, and mascara inside. Makeup did not fit with the Hiking Girl persona I was aspiring to, the type I was sure he liked. I regretted that I didn't know how to whittle.

"I got our tickets already," he said. "I got here sort of early–the F came fast." He was holding a white paper bag and reached inside it. "Coffee?"

"Please." He handed me a cup.

"Blueberry or corn muffin?"

"Blueberry. Thanks."

I reached for my wallet to pay him back, but he said, "Don't worry about it."

"But the tickets–"

"It's on me."

"Thank you," I said, feeling thrilled by his gentlemanliness.

"I packed a bag with sandwiches at home but I forgot to bring it, so we should get lunches for later. We can eat them on top of the mountain," he said. My stomach lurched at the thought of the mountain–we were actually hiking up a mountain. I'd sort of blocked that fact out of my mind.

"There's a deli over there." He pointed, and we went to the tiny counter and bought sandwiches, chips, fruit, and granola bars to eat later.

We stuffed the food into our knapsacks and made our way to the track. Our train was already in the station, its doors open. It was nearly empty. We chose a row and had it all to ourselves.

"How's the wedding planning?" he asked as we settled into our seats, and finished our coffee and muffins.

I rolled my eyes. "Have you heard of Zingy-Dell figurines? Sylvia's obsessed with them. She registered for the entire collection. They're taking over our house."

"Zingy whats?"

"Picture little animals and children clutching signs like 'Smiles' and 'Just Sunshine.' 'Just Sunshine' is a special limited edition, in fact."

"Sounds beautiful."

"The word my sister uses is *batshit.* I think Sylvia's about as different from my mom was as is humanly possible."

He unzipped his blue fleece jacket. "My mom doesn't date much. She used to. Once when I was a kid I took a cat turd out of the litter box and put it in one poor guy's sneaker."

"You didn't."

"The thing was, he wore it for two hours before he said, 'I think there's something in my shoe. . . . '" We both laughed.

A few minutes later I asked, "Where's your father?"

"He died in a car accident the year after I was born."

"That sucks," I said.

"Yup."

The conductor's voice boomed from the PA system, rattling off an unintelligible list of stations. Several more people boarded the train. A minute later it lurched, then grumbled into the bowels of Grand Central.

"You really weren't scared when you were traveling all by yourself?" I asked him.

"Of course I was scared. There was one time I got sick–I thought I was in trouble–but it was just diarrhea."

He said it so casually, tossing it off. *Just diarrhea.* Such an embarrassing word. I couldn't imagine the guys at school saying *just diarrhea* in that soft voice.

"It was lonely sometimes too, but I met a lot of people traveling and made friends. We still write letters. I'm planning to travel again next summer. India, maybe–that's where I'd like to go next. My mom's not exactly overjoyed with the idea–there are more risks of getting secondary infections in third-world countries. But I think I'll wear her down."

He shrugged. He had the same gentle, unflappable tone about this. He yawned, then leaned back and closed his eyes. "You don't mind if I take a nap?"

"I don't mind–I'm tired too."

I loved being this close to him, watching him, his elbow touching mine. I was glad he closed his eyes so I could stare at him blatantly.

I'd had a dream about him the night before. I was hiking with my sister in the Himalayas (though in the dream the mountains looked more like the Abominable Snowman's stomping grounds in Rudolph's Christmas TV specials). As we were trekking through them, we found a place where the earth started to peel off in layers, like old carpet. Underneath the top layer was Sasha, who smiled and said hello; underneath him, in the next layer, was my father, who told us a few bad jokes; beneath that layer was my mother, looking healthy and happy, relaxing in a lounge chair. She hugged us and thanked us for visiting, and said to come back again sometime soon. Then we put the earth back in place.

What did the dream mean? It was different from the Rolf dream–it didn't leave me with questions or confusion. It was just a happy fact: *Oh, there she is, under the earth, same as always.* I'd felt content when I woke up.

My mother would have liked Sasha, I was convinced. His handsomeness, his gentleness, that unassuming calming voice. He looked so healthy, and as I stared at his skin I almost wanted to see scars, some proof or sign of what he'd been through. But he looked fine. You'd never know he had cancer, looking at him. I wanted to ask him what it was like, to know he might die, but I couldn't–it would be the wrong thing to say. It would affect some balance, some unspoken arrangement.

An hour later he blinked awake; he took out a water bottle and offered me a sip. He unfolded a topographical map and showed me where we'd be hiking, and a half hour after that the train pulled into the station. "This is it," he said. We walked down the quaint white station platform and through a tiny town with clapboard houses and immaculate streets, then made a turn onto a country road. It was a quarter mile to the trailhead. A few cars sped by, the drivers staring at us strangely, as if we were homeless people ambling along.

"You don't see a lot of people on the trails here. I think mostly hunters use them." He saw my expression and laughed. "Don't look so scared–it's not hunting season."

We soon reached the trailhead. I was sweating already; I hoped I was in good enough shape for this. But as we started hiking, it didn't seem too bad, though my pretty new maroon sneakers soon looked like they'd been dipped in chocolate cake batter.

I watched him go in front of me. He moved smoothly, more comfortable with his body than I was with mine. He was lithe and graceful as a deer, while I felt awkward, a little too aware of my arms, my legs, my clunky feet.

We hiked past old stone walls and the foundation to a

long-gone home; the forest had taken over, growing inside where the house had once stood. We stopped to check it out. "It's like the Chronicles of Narnia," I said.

"*Prince Caspian*–when they return to that house after all those years and trees have grown up in it?"

I nodded. "I loved that part. It gave me goose bumps." I remembered how it had thrilled and frightened me, the first time I pictured myself as being such a small blip in time.

The trail grew steeper, and I started breathing too hard to talk. I didn't want to go first and have him look at my butt the whole time, but he was hard to keep up with. We stopped for water breaks; he was breathing hard also. Finally, after a long while, the trail leveled off near the top. Then we reached a bare rock incline.

He scrambled up the rock quickly. "Be careful–it's a little slippery," he said.

I tried to place my hands and feet where he had, but I couldn't reach as far. I held on to a root for balance but the root snapped, my foot slid, and I skidded down the rock, landing on my hands and rear end.

"Shit!" My knee was gushing blood, I had a hole in my pants and a huge gash in my leg. My hand was bleeding too.

Sasha climbed down the rock in half a second. "Are you okay?"

"Yeah," I said weakly.

"God–I'm sorry, I should've been spotting you. Can you move your knee okay? Your ankles? Wrists?"

I flexed them all for him. I stood up, a little wobbly, but fine. "I think it's just scrapes," I said.

210

"Sit down–let's clean you up."

We sat below the rock and he took out his first-aid kit. He dabbed antiseptic on to my leg and knee, which stung so badly the word *motherfucker* leaked out of my mouth in a very un-ladylike voice. He applied a huge bandage, then cleaned off my hand too. That didn't hurt so much, him holding my fingertips as he pressed down on the gauze to stop the bleeding.

"It's not so bad," I said, his hand still holding mine.

"You're very brave."

"Ha."

"Do you want to keep going?"

"Of course," I said. I didn't want him to think I was a wimp.

"You sure? We're almost to the top." He let go of my hand. "Then you go first this time–I'll spot you."

It wasn't as romantic as I might have imagined–he egged me on as I sprawled across the rock, clinging to it like a spider. "Put your hand there, and your foot there–that root's not stable . . . there . . . good . . . "

Finally I made it up the rock, and a half hour later we reached the top. The view was fantastic–the huge broad sky, the rolling mountains, and the roads and houses far below, like a toy train model. I was exhausted and exhilarated, sweaty and dirty, relieved and proud.

We ate our sandwiches and lay back on the rocks. After a while the wind made me shiver.

"You cold?"

I had only packed my stylish lightweight black sweater.

"Here." He gave me his fleece jacket.

211

"Don't you need it?"

"I'm fine."

Guys had done this for thousands of years—given girls their jackets (or pelts). But it had never before happened to me.

"It's beautiful," I said, staring at the view, snuggling into the soft jacket, which smelled like laundry detergent and something dark and sweet, like chocolate. "No Himalayas, though."

"Still nice," he said.

"What made you decide to go there, to Nepal? I mean, if there was a risk, like you said . . . "

"I know. Maybe it was stupid. But I was feeling really good, I loved traveling, and I met an Irish couple, Robert and Sue, in a hostel in Amsterdam. They were going and invited me to come. I was reading all these books at the time—that's what I'd do in the hostels at night, and on the trains, read. I'd read Sartre and all this stuff about how you not only choose what to do but who you are . . . and Heidegger, who says it's up to you to make the most of your being . . . and Kierkegaard—at least I think it was Kierkegaard—about beliefs being leaps of faith. I guess I decided I should just take that leap of faith."

"Wow."

He shrugged. "At least that's how I interpreted what they said. I probably got it all wrong."

"But you didn't. You were right to go after all. Don't you think?"

He nodded. "I was." He stood up. "Can you excuse me for a sec? I have to go pee."

I had to also, but I was embarrassed to mention it in front of him, so I went off quietly. It didn't seem like anything would embarrass him. He was so different from guys at school–he didn't care about what clothes you wore or what part of the city you lived in (downtown or Upper West Side, cool; Upper East Side or outer boroughs, uncool). Or if you played ultimate Frisbee (cool) or handball (uncool), or listened to ska (cool) or metal (uncool). All of that seemed on another plane of existence from him. All that was meaningless. Beside the point.

He returned a few minutes later. "It's nice being here with someone else. I love this spot. I think after college I'll move out of the city."

"Where would you go?"

"I don't know. Maybe somewhere abroad."

I felt sad already–nothing had happened between us–and still I felt he shouldn't move abroad.

I watched a bird winging its way through the valley, and hugged my knees under his big jacket. I noticed a dark splotch on the jacket near the zipper. "Oh my God, I'm sorry–I think I got blood on your jacket." I tried to wipe it off, but the stain didn't rub out.

"Don't worry–it's fine. It doesn't matter." He touched my shoulder, and a quiver ran through me.

"I guess a fall like that sort of disputes the 'Everything in nature always works out right' theory," he said.

No, it doesn't, I wanted to say, *not if it made you touch my shoulder right now.*

He surveyed the sky. "We should probably head down–it's going to get dark soon."

We packed up the garbage from our lunches and started to hike down the mountain.

"So what do the other philosophers say about that theory, that nature always works out right?" I asked on the trail.

"I don't know." He held back a branch so it wouldn't snap back toward me. "Honestly, it's hard to keep all their ideas straight. So many of them disagreed with each other, too. I remember Spinoza said matter could think, that all of reality—trees and dirt and rocks and turkey sandwiches—is alive and can know things. Others thought he was crazy." He hopped onto a rock, avoiding a patch of mud. "Plato believed in an ideal world beyond nature—that ideas exist in their own realm, and we don't invent them, we discover them." He paused and leaned against a thick tree. "And he believed that the soul is immortal. Aristotle disagreed—he said the soul is part of the body and dies with it."

"I don't believe that," I said, jumping off a wobbly rock. "I think there is some strange force, or something unexplained, about death. When my mom died we were all there, and at that moment it really felt like passing, like her body was just a shell and her soul was somewhere else, and I wasn't scared. And I feel like she waited for us to be there to die, for the three of us to be in the room with her, even though she wasn't conscious . . . I just feel like there's something we can't explain about it. I've felt her presence at other times too. But sometimes I just don't know, I wonder if maybe I'm just making it all up."

I told him about the dream of my mother, peeling back the layers and finding her there. Except I left out the part about him being in it, not wanting him to think I was obsessed with him.

"Wow. Interesting dream. What do you think it means?"

I climbed over a tree trunk that had fallen across the trail. "I guess . . . I was thinking about it on the ride up. I don't know.

Maybe that . . . love is in layers, or something? Like, you can peel back one and the old loves will still be there. More people you love will accumulate on top, but the old ones stay there, and . . . you can check on them and return to them whenever you want." I smiled and shrugged. "At least, that's sort of the feeling I had when I woke up. This kind of . . . permanent contentment."

We reached the rock where I'd slipped before. I slowly edged down it on my butt. He spotted me from below.

"I don't think it's all over when you die either," he said. "After Nepal I read about Tibetan Buddhism—they see life and death as parts of a whole, and they believe in reincarnation. My mom's also really into these books by this psychiatrist, Elisabeth Kübler-Ross? She worked with dying patients, and she wrote that before she worked with them she didn't believe in life after death, but afterward she did, 'beyond a shadow of a doubt.'"

"I should read her." I paused. "Are you—are you afraid of getting sick again?"

"Sometimes." His voice was harder, more forceful. He snapped off the stem of a wildflower, and I regretted asking. I worried I'd overstepped a boundary or broken the silent arrangement.

We heard crackling branches in the distance and stopped. A fawn pranced across the path, followed by its mother. In a second they were out of sight. We started walking again. The sky was orange through the trees.

"Who's your favorite among all those philosophers?" I asked.

"I'm not sure. I like the Tibetan Buddhists, and the Taoists. They seem sort of similar in ways . . . they both believe

215

that life is about change and impermanence. You're supposed to accept things as they come, focus on what's happening right now, and not let changes upset you, because all things in nature exist in a state of constant flux. Even death isn't a bad thing—it's part of the changes." He hesitated. "I should stop talking about it so much—my mom said it sounds kind of pretentious."

"That's not true," I said. "It doesn't." I loved all this; I drank it in. I'd never had a conversation like this with anyone before.

We'd reached the bottom of the mountain, and the path leveled off and widened.

"How's your hand?" he asked.

"Good. The bleeding stopped."

He picked my hand up in his. I couldn't breathe.

"Your hand is so cold." He warmed it between his palms and held it gently. The forest was dazzling. The failing light dappled the ground with splotches of orange and pink. We walked side by side and he kept holding my hand, gently stroking my fingers. My skin felt damp.

By the time we reached the end of the trail the sky was dark. He got his flashlight out of his backpack and led me to a clearing.

"Here," he said. "This is what I wanted to show you." I looked up. There were millions of stars above us. We stood there, staring at the sky, my hand still in his.

"I like you very much," he said after a while.

No one had ever come out and said that to me before. I didn't know what to say in return. *Me too* sounded wrong, as did *So do I.* Finally I said, "I like you." I thought we might kiss, though he made no move to lean toward me–but that was fine too. *I could stay here, silent, my hand in his always,* I thought.

In romance novels this would change everything. A hand holding on page fifteen and you knew for certain, no matter what, that the couple would end up together, that not even 350 pages of pirates, wars, family deception, or evil twins could keep them apart.

That's what I liked about those books. I wanted to believe when I read them that that kind of love was possible and real, that it truly existed.

And it wasn't only romance novels, either–I'd read *A Room with a View* after seeing the movie with Kelsey. We'd copied an E. M. Forster quote onto the back cover of our denim notebook binders: *It isn't possible to love and to part.*

I didn't want to go, but he turned, still holding my hand, and said, "Are you hungry? Should we stop and get something in town?"

"Okay." I didn't care about food or anything. We walked toward town, still holding hands.

We found a small restaurant called Billy's Steaks and Chops, which had red-checkered plastic tablecloths and bright red booths. We sat in one and ordered hamburgers and Sprites. The conversation switched to lighter things–TV shows, the worst subways, his mother's obsession with their cat.

On the Metro-North home I leaned on his shoulder and slept. Pretended to sleep. He kept his arm around me, and I was sure I'd never felt so happy. I thought of *A Room with a View* again, of George and Lucy leaning over the river Arno, and George saying, *Something tremendous has happened.* And George's father telling Lucy later: *He is already part of you.*

At Grand Central he walked me to the 7 train–it was pulling into the station, and we ran to meet it. He held the door open; we hugged quickly, he kissed me swiftly on the cheek, and I hopped inside the car.

The doors closed and the train barreled home.

I sat on the gray seat and replayed the whole day in my mind. On the back of a loose-leaf sheet where I'd written the time we were meeting, I transcribed everything in my head– the "I like you very much," the hand holding, the philosophy. I wanted to remember it, all of it, to not forget a single moment of the whole day. I was certain I'd never felt so happy before. My body was singing with it.

My dad and Sylvia were in the kitchen when I walked in. "How was your day? And evening?" my dad asked.

"Fine."

He was cleaning up from dinner, rinsing off plates and loading them into the dishwasher. Sylvia was seated at the kitchen table, drying off a gaudy flowered bowl–an engagement gift, I figured.

"Gigi called," my dad said.

"Yeah?"

"She said Sasha left his lunch at home today. He forgot it."

"Oh." So I'd lied–so what? I didn't care–I was flying.

"You had a nice time hiking?" my dad asked.

I took my knapsack off my shoulder. "I had a nice time."

"Why didn't you tell us you were going on a trip with him?"

"It wasn't a *trip*–it was just a hike. It's not a big deal." I started to walk out of the kitchen.

"We'd like to talk about it," he said. "Sylvia and I have been discussing it."

I paused. Sylvia got up from the kitchen table and started packing leftovers into Ziploc bags. She didn't make eye contact with me.

"You've been *discussing* it?" I asked.

"We don't think this is wise," he said.

"What?"

"We don't think it's wise to be dating Sasha." He said this more to the dishwasher than to me.

"What are you talking about?" This wasn't dating–dating was stupid girls and boys twittering in TV sitcoms. It couldn't be more different from what had just happened between Sasha and me. "We're not *dating*. And why do you care?" I scratched my bruised leg.

He noticed the gash on my hand, the hole in my pant leg. "What happened there?"

"Nothing."

Sylvia put her Ziploc bags into the fridge. "He's quite a few years older than you, and he's–it's just not healthy," she said, not looking at me.

"What? What's not healthy?"

"We want to protect you," she said. "He's very sick. Leukemia is not a joke."

"I don't give a shit about that," I said.

She winced. "And he's very reckless–"

219

"We don't want to see your heart broken," my father said.

"Well, it already is broken, all right? Permanently. There's nothing you can do about *that*." I was thinking of my mother, and thinking of her made me angrier.

"You've had enough tragedy for your sixteen years," he continued. "Enough loss for your age."

"So what? Who gives a fuck? I can lose whoever I want!" I couldn't believe I was saying this. What was I saying? What were *they* saying? And what did any of it have to do with Sasha? I gaped at them, half doubting that this was actually going on.

"Please. Don't get upset. We just don't think you should go on another date with him again. That's all," my father said.

"We? *We*?" I glared at Sylvia's back as she silently packed vegetables into Tupperware containers. I knew this was all her doing. My father liked Sasha–I knew that.

"You're being crazy. *You* like him. What does it matter what *she* thinks?" I asked him.

He banged the dishwasher door closed. "That's enough."

Sylvia continued to pack the vegetables. "We both don't trust him with you," she said calmly. "He's going to take advantage."

"What?" I sputtered. "You don't know *what*–I mean, Sasha is–and compared to–" I wanted to tell her about Felix, and the difference between Felix and Sasha, but I didn't want to bring that up. "And Mommy would've loved Sasha! I know she would! And this is none of *your* goddamn business!"

My father turned sharply and yelled, "Oh it's very much her business! You listen to her. She's a member of this family now, of this house. What she says goes!" He pointed an accusing finger at me.

That got me. *Our* house. Spooky House. *My* house. The house she'd invaded and ruined.

"Fuck you!" I screamed, and the next thing I knew I was at the hall cabinet with Just Sunshine in one hand and Keep on Truckin' in the other, and I smashed them both on the kitchen floor as hard as I could.

Silence.

We stared in shock. I thought I should say *Fuck you!* again for emphasis, though I felt sorry seeing Sylvia's bare, hurt face, watching her gather up the shards and pieces, examining them, seeming like she might cry. I couldn't look at her. I ran upstairs and shut the door to my room. I cried a few tears, which I told myself were over my mother. And it didn't matter what they'd said about Sasha, I told myself. I'd see him anyway. They had no control. They didn't run the subway system. I could see him whenever I wanted.

But as I lay there thinking, a flicker of doubt rose in me: the fear that the romance novels and E. M. Forster were wrong, that in reality it was very possible and in fact likely to love and to part. Not from being forbidden to see him, or his disease, but a million other countless, endless ways–traveling to other countries, meeting other people, going to college, growing older. He could simply change his mind; he could wake up one day and feel differently. And that would be that.

I took out the loose-leaf paper, my transcription of the day, my tiny writing, wavy from the rocking subway, and read it, and reread it, to remember what I'd felt with his arm around me on the train. I kept reading until I fell asleep.

My father woke me up in the middle of the night.

"I'm taking Sylvia to the hospital."

"What's wrong?"

"I'm not sure. Don't worry. I'll call you when we get there. Go back to sleep."

Sylvia died at four in the morning. My father called me at six and told me over the phone. He was still at the hospital. She'd had a stroke. "An ischemic stroke," he said. There was a possibility it had been caused by her drug treatment; no one was sure.

My throat dried up. "It's my fault," I said.

"It's not your fault. You had nothing to do with it." His voice sounded dry and crackly, impatient and exhausted. "I'm going to go to Sylvia's apartment to make the calls. You can come over when you're ready. I called Alex–she's taking a bus home this morning. Felix was just here–he left a few minutes ago."

"Is he okay?" I asked.

"Not so good. He's on his way to a friend's."

"Daddy–I feel terrible."

"I do too."

"It's my fault."

"Stop it. I'll see you later."

I didn't go to Sylvia's. I got dressed and took the F train to Brooklyn, to the Carroll Street stop near Sasha's house. I cried on the subway, which was empty except for one man who said, "Doll, if he's that bad, you did the right thing to leave him." I was still crying when Sasha opened the door.

"What happened?" He blinked; he'd been asleep. His hair was matted to his face and he had a crease from a pillow, like a scar, running down one cheek.

"Sylvia died. I killed her." Through tears I told him about the fight, leaving out the parts about him; I said it was a spat that had gone out of control. I didn't want him to know what my father and Sylvia had said, but I hoped he might comfort me, or calm my fears, or just listen.

He sat down on the stoop and put his arm around me. It was chilly out, but he was in shorts and a gray sweatshirt, and his feet were bare. I stared at his wide naked toes.

The front door opened and Gigi joined us on the stoop. She held her yellow satin robe closed at the front. "What happened? Is everything okay?"

"Sylvia died," Sasha said.

"Oh, my God." She leaned on the railing. "Jesus Christ. I'm so sorry. What—what can I do? Does your dad–?"

"I think he's okay," I said. "I mean, he sounded . . . I think he's okay. He's making phone calls."

"Oh, God." She shook her head and hugged her elbows. "I'm going to get dressed. Sasha—make the poor girl some coffee. I'm so sorry, hon. Jesus. Come inside, okay?" She bent and kissed my head, rubbed her hand on my back, and disappeared into the house.

"Do you want some coffee?" Sasha asked.

"No. Thanks."

Then he said, "You didn't kill her because you smashed her figurine."

"Yes. I did. Figurines—two figurines. Just Sunshine and Keep on Truckin'. The Just Sunshine actually wasn't that bad. The bear was sort of cute."

What I didn't tell him was that deep inside, a part of me had secretly wished her death—I'd never come right out and admitted that to myself, but hadn't I had a nagging hope that their marriage might not happen, that something would interfere and stop it? Hadn't I resented her living with cancer while my mom had died? And the wish had come true. I stared at my new maroon sneakers, the mud still caked on from our hike.

"I'm sure the medication had something to do with it, like your dad said—those chemo drugs can kill you."

"No. It was me. I mean, the stress from the fight—and maybe all those feelings I had. I mean, she knew I didn't like her—and I think deep inside I wanted—"

"Believe me, you don't have that much power." He shook his head and made a strange sound, a muffled, mournful laugh.

I felt shamed then. He was right—it was presumptuous to think I was the sole culprit, that I could give life or take it away. How self-important. How obnoxious. But I was certain I'd played some part in it . . . and I deserved punishment. Something would be taken from me.

"My dad," I said, thinking aloud. The doctors had been

frightened for his health after losing one wife. And now he'd lost two.

He squeezed my shoulder. "Your dad will be okay," he said softly.

"How do you know that?"

He didn't answer.

Even if my dad was okay, he wouldn't forget this. "He says he doesn't blame me, but he's never going to forgive me for that fight. I mean, it was her last night." I wiped my nose and tried not to cry again.

"He'll forgive you. I did."

"What? For what?"

"I wasn't going to tell you this." He paused, took his arm off my shoulder, and gazed across the street. "I overheard, at NYU once, you and your sister calling me 'the cancer guy.' I think you thought I was sleeping and couldn't hear you."

I inhaled and held my breath. It was confirmed, it was true: I was a horrible person. I remembered the derogatory way we'd said it. *Cancer guy.* Funny. Ha ha ha. Unlucky him.

"It's all right. I've heard worse," he said.

"Oh my God. You must hate me." My face flushed with humiliation.

"I was annoyed at the time–but I know that's not who you are."

I wanted to sink under the stoop, to disappear. A door opened across the street; a man came out in boxer shorts, his huge belly flowing over his waistband. He picked up his newspaper and waved at us. Sasha waved back.

I noticed goose bumps on Sasha's legs. "I should go," I said. "You're cold, you should go inside, and I–"

"Come on, come inside–I'll make you some coffee."

"No . . ." I wanted to leave, to forget that this had happened, to go back in time to yesterday, the hike, the complete glee I'd felt on the train home, that now seemed years ago.

"Come on." He picked up my hand, opened the door, and led me upstairs. Gigi was in the shower, and the coffee was already brewing.

"I think Morty Grossman just hit on me," Alex said at the reception Tuesday evening. We'd just come from the funeral and the cemetery; we'd cleaned up our house for the occasion, ordered food, and arranged the flowers. When my father had informed the wedding florist of what had happened, she'd sent several tremendous arrangements. Our house was filled with lilacs.

"How could Morty Grossman hit on you? What did he say?"

"He was leering at me over his walker."

"I think that's how he always looks. Daddy said he's almost blind." I picked at my pumpernickel bagel. "You would make a nice couple, though."

"Thanks. As do you and the cancer guy."

"Don't call him that. I told you. It's mean."

"See? You *like* him. That's okay. I like him too. I can't believe he's doing the dishes."

I glanced into the kitchen, where Sasha and Gigi and Kelsey were arranging desserts on trays and washing cleared plates. We'd tried to stop them; they shooed us out and forbade us to help. I watched him lean over the sink, his hair falling into his eyes. It thrilled me to look at him. He still liked me, it seemed. I couldn't believe it. After the episode on his stoop Sunday morning, we'd had breakfast and he'd walked me to the subway, holding my hand. He'd hugged me good-bye for a long time, kissing my head and my cheek and, very briefly, my lips. It had been so quick I'd practically missed it. Did that count as a real kiss? I hoped it counted.

I wanted to kiss him. For real.

Alex eyed me. "Get your mind out of the gutter."

"What?"

"You're gawking at him," she said. She knew all about the fight and the figurine smashing, and a few details of our hiking excursion. I hadn't told her everything; I hadn't told anyone how much I really liked him, not even Kelsey. I wanted to protect it, curl around it, these strange raw vulnerable feelings.

"I don't think Felix likes you, though," she said, bringing me back to Earth. "He was looking at you earlier with this odd expression on his face. Like—a sneer, almost."

"What?"

I'd never told her about the Felix episode.

She shrugged, glancing at Felix in the yard, through the window. He was talking to a crowd of his fashion industry friends, a cigarette in one hand and a drink in the other. Alex sighed and surveyed the living room.

Our house was packed with people. My father had called everyone from the wedding invitation list. There were mostly people I didn't know—Sylvia's neighbors and friends, the wedding coordinator at Briar Manor, the rabbi who'd been going to marry them. My father brought Omi and Opa, my mother's parents, too. They seemed to have no idea what was going on. They sat on our sofa and smiled absently at Alex and me. There were some of the same people who had come to my mother's funeral also: our neighbors, the Lillys and Lombardis; my kindergarten teacher, Mrs. Lowery; and Lottie Silverberg, our old babysitter.

"Déjà vu," Alex said, glancing around the crowd.

"Yeah," I said. I scratched my back; my new wool dress itched. "I still feel guilty."

"You should. You killed her."

"That's not funny."

"If you really believed you did, then you wouldn't be smiling."

I rubbed the point of my shoe on the floor. "I guess. Still— no more joking about that."

"Fine." We watched our father talk to Lottie nearby. "How's Daddy doing, you think?" she asked.

"I don't know."

His voice was loud and overpowering. "Very nice, every deposit refunded. We still have to return the gifts," he was telling her. Lottie said something I couldn't hear, and he nodded. "She helped me get over Greta's death. She'd lost husbands. She said she was a pro. She said, 'At first, you're sad all the time. But then you're sad occasionally.'" Lottie said something else inaudible, and then my dad said, "I'm waiting for occasionally."

I felt a hand on my shoulder and turned. It was Felix. "*Mama mia* Mia Mia," he drawled. He was completely smashed, or stoned, or both. I smiled at him briefly and turned back to Alex, hoping he'd go away.

"What? You're not talkin' to me? Mia Mia Mia Mia!" he shouted; several people stopped and stared.

He looked like he was about to do something; Kelsey appeared at my side.

"Fresh air," she said to Felix. "I think you could use some fresh air. Have you seen the lovely backyard?"

Felix gazed at Kelsey. "Yer pretty."

"Good to hear it," she said, leading him out the door.

Sasha appeared too. "Everything okay?" He touched my shoulder.

"I think so," I said. I saw Felix back with his friends in the yard.

Sasha unrolled his shirtsleeves. "I need to run out–we're out of half-and-half," he said.

"I'll go to the store," Alex said. "I need a break."

"Want me to come?" I asked her.

"No–I'll be fine." She smirked.

"What?"

"Your taste has improved since Jay Kasper."

Shut up was lingering on my tongue, but I held it back, not wanting to say it in front of Sasha. Alex winked at me like a bad comedy skit and left.

"Who?" Sasha asked.

"Oh, never mind."

"You could use a break too," Sasha said. "How about an escape to the roof?"

"Good idea." I hadn't been on our roof in ages. I wanted to

be alone with him, to be away from everybody else. I watched him walk in front of me up the stairs, his strong legs in creased black pants. On the second floor of our house I showed him the ladder, next to the bathroom.

He climbed up and moved the heavy hatch door. An old woman waiting outside the bathroom glanced up, muttered, "*Meshugeneh,*" and looked away.

He was on the roof already, staring down at me. "Coming up?"

I managed to get up the ladder even with my heels on, pressing my insteps on each rung. He helped me scramble over the top edge and onto the tarry black surface, holding my hand. The trees shimmered around its edges. An airplane like a moving glowing star roamed above.

"Wow," he said, seeing the view of Manhattan. It was different from the view from Brooklyn; midtown was more prominent from here, with the Chrysler and Citicorp buildings, and the Empire State Building was lit up in blue tonight. We stood at the roof's edge. The buildings looked so near it seemed you could reach out and run your hands across their silky glass.

"How are you?" he asked.

"I'm okay. Much better."

He smiled that warm, direct grin. It felt strange seeing him in our house, our private home, unrecognizable with the people and food and flowers.

He bent toward me, placing his hands on the sides of my face until I was looking straight at him. He kissed me. His lips were warm and firm, and my brain started searching for

230

adjectives, to record every millimeter of this kiss, its imprint, its history, to preserve it forever. *Warm, wet, strong.* The adjectives floated, as did my entire body, pressing into his, thinking, *I want to be you. I want to stay like this.*

Something in me hesitated.

"What is it? What's wrong?" he asked.

"Nothing."

"The kiss? I'm a bad kisser."

"You're not—you're very, very good." I held his hand and felt the thin skin of his wrist under my fingers. "I was just thinking that I wish we could stay like this—that it wasn't all a constant state of change or whatever." I was thinking once more of the future—college, other countries, other people, growing older, losing him.

He paused and touched my shoulder. "Maybe that's not the whole story, though. It could be—or maybe it's like your dream."

I smiled. "You mean in five or twenty years I can peel back the earth like a layer of carpet, and we'll still be here on the roof?"

He didn't answer. He kissed me again and wrapped his arms around me. His shirt smelled dark and sweet, like his jacket on the mountain. My insides began to lift as he held me, his hands tracing circles softly on my back, my stomach pressed to his, my face resting on his chest.

Everything changed. I knew that. Then why did I feel some trickle of hope, some blind, faithful belief telling me that what I felt at sixteen I would feel forever? That this feeling might stay here on this roof, wrapped up like a package, like the packages of love for my mother that dwelled in the house below our feet, in every room, every closet, in its very walls and furniture and floors and air?

If grief had a permanence, then didn't also love?

We stood on the roof, under the starless sky, standing still.

Afterword

MY MOTHER DIED on January 26, 1991, of melanoma, nine days after the diagnosis. I was a few years older than Mia, but her feelings of grief on these pages are based on what I experienced.

I started writing this book five years after my mother died, and completed the first draft in two years. A month later, my father died of a heart attack. He was very much like the father in this book–he'd had two previous heart attacks, and triple bypass surgery when I was fifteen–and we'd become extremely close in the years after my mother died. Despite having spent ages thinking and writing about grief, despite believing I'd shone a light in every corner of the experience of losing a parent, I was devastated by his death. What was the point of writing about it anymore? What was there to say about loss except that it sucked, that I was depressed and miserable and missed my father and mother and wanted them back? Even my working title seemed to mock me: *Cures for Heartbreak.* I put the draft aside.

Having already endured the heartbreak of losing my mother, I knew what I was in for after I lost my father. I thought of the countless nights I'd wished I could call her and tell her about a breakup with a boyfriend or about failing a class at school, and the leafy feeling in my stomach when I realized I couldn't; I thought of how my heart would almost squeeze itself out of my chest every time I saw a girl and her mother on the escalator at Bloomingdale's or casually sipping coffee together in a café on Mother's Day; already I couldn't bear to even walk by Wendy's, the site of so many grilled chicken sandwiches shared with my father. My father's death only seemed to compound the grief I still felt for my mother. I felt a sense of dislocation so severe I sometimes felt seasick, as if I'd stepped onto a ship's deck in a storm and couldn't find the door to go back inside. I was prone to dramatic statements such as "I guess I can never get married now, since neither of them will be there at my wedding"—even though at the time there wasn't a husband, much less a boyfriend, anywhere in sight. But I was certain of my future just the same.

Years passed. The waves of seasickness became less frequent. I finally began to feel ready to work on this book again. Four years after my father died, I met a man (he's gentle and sweet, with a character similar to Sasha's), we fell in love, he asked me to marry him, and lo and behold, we decided to have a wedding. A week before the event, as I was preparing to leave for Vermont—we'd planned a weekend wedding outside, near a lake—I started to cry. It seemed an unbelievable mistake, an omission, that here I was marrying the love of my life, and my parents wouldn't be there. How had this happened? How could I possibly get married without them? What was I doing? Would they approve? Would they like my soon-to-be husband? How could neither of them be there to walk me down the aisle?

I cried for a while, and then my sister (who had the bad luck to get a writer for a sister, since she's been forced to endure her friends' saying, whenever they've read excerpts of this book published in magazines, "I feel like I know you so much better!" So I have to say: she's nothing like Alex. Really. No likeness whatsoever. Even if she disdains makeup and loves hiking boots and we still argue perpetually over whether the 46th Street or 52nd Street subway station was closer to our house) calmed me down a little, and we drove to Vermont together. Unfortunately, my spirits only grew darker once I saw the weather reports for our outdoor event: rain, and lots of it.

Then, the day of the wedding, a half hour before the ceremony, the clouds retreated. The sky turned unfathomably blue. My sister walked me down the aisle, and the rabbi read a quote from the Book of Zohar, which says that when a parent has died God personally invites him or her under the chuppah, the wedding canopy.

I've never felt my parents' presence as strongly as I did that day. I'm certain they were with us, under the chuppah, on the green hill overlooking the lake.

It doesn't mean that I'm over their deaths, that I will ever get over them. In some ways I'm still that girl crying on the subway platform or in the hospital bathroom; I'm still the girl who has a brick in her chest every time she sees a daughter shopping with her mother in Bloomingdale's and whenever she walks by Wendy's. And at the same time I am grateful that I had my parents as long as I did, and that I can keep them alive in a dream, at a wedding, in a story.

Acknowledgments

THANK YOU TO my phenomenal agent, Jennifer Rudolph Walsh, for believing in me for many years, and to her fantastic assistants, Daria Cercek and Shannon Firth. I'm indebted to my wonderful editors at Random House, Beverly Horowitz and Jodi Keller, for their insightful editing, and for suggesting that I write the afterword.

Thank you also to the magazine editors who were willing to pick a new writer out of the slush pile, and who first published parts of this book: C. Michael Curtis at the *Atlantic Monthly;* Ben Schrank, Darcy Jacobs, Melanie Mannarino, and Tamara Glenny at *Seventeen;* Linda Swanson-Davies and Susan Burmeister-Brown at *Glimmer Train Stories;* R. T. Smith at *Shenandoah;* Hannah Tinti and Maribeth Batcha at *One Story;* and Alan Davis and Michael White at *American Fiction.* I'm grateful to the people who read early drafts, especially Anna Sabat Wolin, Allison Moore, and Becky Hagenston. Thank you to my friends Julien Yoo, Elizabeth Everett, Pinckney Benedict, Steve Almond, Robin Lauzon, Matt Modica, Dan Elish, Devon Holmes, Amy Murphy, Valerie

Greenhill, Leslie Pietrzyk, Merrill Feitell, Sarah Squire, and Helen Reid for all their support and encouragement. I'm lucky to be a part of the best community of writers anyone could ask for: the Delta Schmelta Sorority, otherwise known as Dika Lam, Lara JK Wilson, Allison Amend, and Sheri Joseph.

Large sections of this book were written at the MacDowell Colony, and I thank everyone I met there during repeated stays, especially the staff, who have built a magical place where creative work feels important and necessary. Thank you also to the following organizations, which provided time, places, and encouragement to write: the University of Arizona's Creative Writing Program, the Bread Loaf Writers' Conference, the Sewanee Writers' Conference, the Virginia Center for the Creative Arts, and the Djerassi Resident Artists Program.

I owe a huge debt of gratitude to my sister, Jackie, who is such a part of these pages, and who puts up with my writing about our family and is willing to love me anyway. And to my husband, Marshall Reid, for taking my broken heart and putting it back together again.